A Plague of Sailors

It is just before dawn in a remote Highland glen. At the main gate of what seems to be a hydro-electric station lounges the bored watchman, counting the minutes before he comes off duty. The headlights of a distant car are the only touch of life in a tranquil scene. And then . . .

And then we are pitchforked into one of the most sensational adventure stories of the last decade, in which germ warfare is harnessed to the needs of a gang of ruthless fanatics. A merchant vessel ploughing across the Mediterranean with a cargo of grain for earthquake-racked Israel; ambush and murder on the high seas; the transformation of eight thousand tons of grain into eight thousand tons of golden murder; a dramatic ramming which leaves the reader almost as breathless as the protagonists; the final explosive dénouement with its bitter ironical twist: in A PLAGUE OF SAILORS the stakes are the lives of a whole nation and the risks are proportionally high.

After his astonishingly successful début with A FLOCK OF SHIPS everyone wondered whether Brian Callison could do it again. He has not; he has done far, far more.

Brian Callison

A Plague of
Sailors

Collins
St James's Place, London

William Collins Sons & Co Ltd
London · Glasgow · Sydney · Auckland
Toronto · Johannesburg

First published 1971
© Brian Callison
ISBN 0 00 221654 X
Set in Monotype Caslon
Made and Printed in Great Britain by
William Collins Sons & Co Ltd Glasgow

The Happening

The sign on the heavy mesh gates said simply –

NORTH OF SCOTLAND HYDRO-ELECTRIC BOARD
GLEN DHEARG HIGH TENSION RESEARCH STATION

but, strung at twenty foot intervals along the high wire fence climbing straight as a ski-tow up the mountain-side, ancillary boards stated with perhaps more impact on the cynically venturesome –

N.O.S.H.E.B.

UNRESTRICTED GUARD DOG OPERATION
DO NOT PASS THIS POINT OR YOU
MAY BE KILLED!

No further amplification was in evidence to inform the, by now presumably deterred, trespasser on whether the threat loomed from a million volt arc or a predatory Canis Familiaris.

Certainly the two men lounging just inside the gate didn't appear exceptionally aware of N.O.S.H.E.B.'s promise of a supercharged Armageddon. Only of the sheer monotony of facing a few stringy yellow sheep browsing disconsolately through the heather, flanked by a geometrically menacing row of notices stretching to infinity.

7

The older man shifted the shotgun he was holding to a more comfortable lie in the crook of his other arm and glanced briefly back down the rutted track that wound, as if accidentally, round the dark shoulder of the mountain. Noticing the suspended veil of rain fuzzing the underside of the black storm clouds he turned back to glower at the sheep.

'Bastards!' he said ambiguously, more in resignation than in malice.

The young one pretended the toe of his boot was a bulldozer and engulfed a scurrying ant under an avalanche of peat dust. Somehow the burnished toe-cap seemed out of keeping with the image of a tweed-suited Hydro Board employee, but it was a small point, hardly noticeable to the casual observer.

'A proper bastard, Corporal,' he agreed after due consideration.

Which was another strange thing because, while the North of Scotland Hydro Board have linesmen and charge-hands and gaffers, they don't have any corporals – with or without boots to grace a guardsman.

Or a military policeman?

Corporal peered at his watch, at the same time deriving a certain bloody-minded satisfaction from observing the ant struggle, erratically victorious, from its temporary entombment.

'Coming up to zero five hundred.'

'Better make the post report then.' The bulldozer disinterestedly squashed the ant flat to win the game.

Corporal turned irritably towards the door of the

little gate hut, then swung back and waved the shotgun authoritatively. 'Mind an' not open them gates while I'm inside, laddie. Not for anyone.'

He stepped into the hut while Bulldozer gave him a surreptitious soldier's farewell and glanced cynically both ways down to where the glen road faded into the grey half-light of approaching dawn. Just for a fleeting moment he thought he saw a yellow glow swell and fade at the head of the valley but it was probably a mistake. No one ever came through Glen Dhearg, not until the tourist season opened next month or so. Corporal was dead right, it was a definite bastard.

Inside the hut Corporal lit an Embassy Tipped and reached for the field telephone in the chipped grey-green case. He twirled the generator handle viciously, hoping like hell the duty men at Control were close enough to their receiver to receive the full traumatic impact of its high-pitched shriek.

He grinned as he heard the handset being snatched off almost immediately, and Tallow's plaintive voice on the other end. 'Duty Room. Staff Tallow!'

'Main gate, Alfa Zulu. Checking in. All correct.'

Tallow hadn't forgotten his rude awakening. 'All correct what, Corporal Grey?'

Provost Corporal Grey, for that was his name, stuck two fingers up at the phone. 'All correct, *Staff* Sergeant.'

See what I mean? he thought. They dress you up like a cross between a civil bloody servant an' a bulled-up Highland ghillie. They swop your 9mm. Sterling

for a twelve bore fuggin' pheasant gun. They tell you
never to go near, or even talk about, the big granite
building over the hill that looks like – but isn't – an
electricity sub-station. They tell you those gates out
there must never, repeat never, be opened unless for
the bearer of a Red Tango Sierra clearance. They tell
you to act like a Hydro Board squaddie when the only
electrical thing for miles is that bloody overworked
kettle in the duty room . . .

. . . but you still got to say '*Staff* Sergeant' to a bloody
staff sergeant!

The receiver crackled again. 'Dogs on circuit,
Corporal?'

Grey hesitated briefly. That was a point. He had four
dogs working the perimeter trained to lope after one
another when unleashed at ten minute intervals, which
meant that each beast should complete its tour of the
wire within forty minutes – one past the gate every ten.
But his attention had wandered, he couldn't remember
seeing any of them since, say, four thirty-five?

Oh Christ! Steady mate; keep the heid, like they'd
say down in the village. Just get Tallow off the line then
check yourself . . .

'Affirmative, Staff Sergeant,' he said. 'Workin' like a
railway timetable.'

He heard Tallow sniff along half a mile of field cable.
'Then you nearly got yourself on a charge f'r a start,
Grey. An' them things of yours – they're not dogs,
they're bloody werewolves. What d'you handlers do for
leave, spend it in the bloody jungle?'

The corporal grinned worriedly, itching to get off the phone. 'Dodgier than that, Staff. I got a depraved bird who's married to a Navy inter-divisional boxin' champion. It's like Russian roulette, but with sex.'

He hung up quickly and half turned towards the door just as Bulldozer's cropped skull poked through. 'Vehicle approachin' from the left,' the ant-killer said.

Grey picked up the twelve bore and stepped out into the monochrome Highland dawn, eyes searching anxiously along the perimeter wire for a movement to betray the position of his wayward prowlers. Maybe they've gone after a hare, he thought? Or even a deer? But he knew they hadn't. They were only interested in people. He shivered involuntarily, suddenly he sensed that things weren't right.

'Goin' like a bloody bomb,' Bulldozer muttered interestedly. Anything was better than staring hypnotically at those goddamned tattered Scotch sheep, even an anonymous car travelling along a road that hardly felt the tread of a Michelin X from one day's end to another.

The corporal allowed his eyes to rest briefly on the warm yellow glow of the approaching headlights. Still a couple of miles away. Probably risking a broken spring as a short cut through the glen to the A 836 north of Caley ... what the hell, where were those bastard dogs? He pulled a dog call from his pocket and blew silently and urgently into it.

Nothing moved along the fence as the first drops of rain pattered whisperingly into the heather.

'I'm going to check with the Pill Box,' Grey muttered, strangely frightened. 'You call me if you see them bloody dogs.'

Bulldozer shrugged and, as Grey disappeared inside the hut again, glanced back along the service road that wound round the side of the mountain. You had to admit that whoever originally set up the Pill Box had done a bloody good job. Only the slightest protuberance in a naturally broken skyline indicated where it was sited, while even a search through powerful glasses wouldn't reveal the bracken-camouflaged apertures which allowed a 120 degree arc of fire to back up the doggy men cum mufti guards on Alfa Zulu main gate.

A diesel-injected rumble reached him faintly from the northern end of the glen and he turned in surprise. *Two* vehicles passing through Dhearg at once? And at five a.m.? Jeeze but the Highlands and Islands Development Board must be doing a bloody smart promotion job. But they wouldn't be advertising what was happening in that big building on the backside of Ben Dhearg, not unless they wanted the biggest scandal to hit Scotland since James the First got His at Flodden. Or was it that Charlie . . . ?

He forgot about looking for the corporal's dogs and idly tried to guess which converging set of headlights was going to pass the gates first.

The bulled-up toe cap stubbed casually around, trying to scare up a few more ants.

*

Grey put down the phone and bit his lip anxiously. So they couldn't see his dogs from the Pill Box either? And they couldn't have cared bloody less anyway. Lucky bastards, all nice an' cosy in a fug of tobacco smoke along with their heavy machine gun, hot coffee flask and their bacon sandwiches conned out've the cook corporal. Christ, it wasn't duty for the M.G. section, it was a Highland holiday.

He stepped out of the hut, blinked fretfully in the glare of swathing headlights as they rounded the last bend then – suddenly – it was all happening!

A fleeting impression of a pantechnicon shape bearing in from the right, a screaming torment of braking rubber culminating in a terrifying bang, and a little blue Volkswagen careering madly out of control until it brought up, half on its side, in the ditch directly across from the main gates.

Then as abruptly as it began, the noise ceased. All movement ceased. And the big pantechnicon sat, angled and still, across the road while the little blue car silently directed twin Laser-like beams of light to blind the gunners in the Pill Box.

And Bulldozer looked, dead shattered, at Grey and said, 'Jesus Christ!' while the corporal, shocked now as well as frightened, answered, 'Don't you open them bloody gates f'r God's sake. I'll phone for assistance.'

Until slowly, almost dreamily, the driver's door of the Volkswagen swung open and a girl fell out into the road and lay there with long, shapely legs still inverted into the car. And she started to scream. Shrilly, and horribly, and unbearably.

Bulldozer said 'Oh, *Jesus* Christ!' again and fumbled with shaking hands at the heavy bolts on the gate, but Corporal Grey didn't try to stop him this time. He couldn't. Instead he just gripped the shotgun desperately, and wished his dogs were with him, and stared with a disturbingly sexual awareness at the grotesquely splayed thighs of the screaming girl.

He saw Bulldozer run across the road, then the girl started to writhe hideously and the kid stopped and flapped his hands helplessly and said, 'Please Miss. Don't move . . . Please Miss.'

He wasn't aware of the men piling out of the big van's offside door until he heard an odd slamming noise to his left, and Bulldozer stopped flapping his hands and put them up to his head. Then blood spurted out between the already dead fingers and spattered over the shiny toe caps.

A little voice in Grey's brain kept sobbing 'You *knew* you shouldn't have opened them fuggin' gates!' while all the time he was swinging fast, the shotgun barrels vectoring on to the group of running men. But he knew it was too late for self-reproach when he saw the automatic rifle with the fold-over shoulder stock and the burr walnut grip already lined up on his belly.

Strangely, the last conscious impression Provost Corporal Grey retained during the milli-seconds it took for four 7.62 millimetre Russian short rounds to stitch a diagonal perforation from right hip to left shoulder, was 'What a bloody lovely pair of legs that dolly's go...'

But then, that was why Provost Corporal Grey was still only a corporal!

*

Inside the hut the grey-green telephone started to scream – just as the girl beside the car stopped.

Ignoring it, the man with the Model 58 Czechoslovak gas-operated rifle stepped quickly over to where the corporal's body had been propelled by the slightest pressure of his finger. A brief glance at the obscenely flowering chest cavity was enough and he turned away as the long legged girl came up beside him. Their eyes held for a moment until she could see her sadness reflected, while he felt the fingertips gently brush the back of his hand as he gazed along the beam of the Volkswagen lights, now diffusing into the opaqueness of the coming day. The mountain was still a jet black two-dimensional cut-out and he calculated that, for a few more minutes, the glare from the so carefully crashed car would blind the men in the Pill Box.

Angling his watch he caught the light from behind – 5.23 a.m. One hundred more seconds and they would have to move according to the plan of attack, even if it meant a frontal assault on the M.G. post which would kill them before they got to within a hundred yards. He bit his lip and allowed his eyes to travel proudly over the ring of commandos fanning out around him, each one in the prone position, weapons covering a

360 degree arc, and all waiting in disciplined silence. All waiting for the death they knew might be very near. But not until . . .

The telephone in the little hut stopped shrieking with heart-clutching abruptness.

*

Provost Staff Sergeant Tallow was angry. Bloody angry.

And dead nervous.

He relinquished the useless generator handle that should have been waking the dead down at Alfa Zulu and waited tensely for Lance-corporal Ellis to finish his cryptic conversation over the other phone. Ellis slammed down the receiver and looked at him apprehensively.

'They can't see a bloody thing from the Pill Box, Staff,' Ellis said. 'All they know is that some clown seems to have piled up on the glen road so that they're dazzled by headlights. It's still too dark to get a sitrep. Then they said . . . they said . . .'

Ellis ground to an uncertain halt and tried to smile, ruggedly disbelieving, like they did on the films. But Tallow was starting to feel scared. Too bloody scared to waste time coaxing a would-be hard man like Ellis. He slammed his hand flat on the table.

'Don't bugger me about, Ellis!' he ground viciously.

Ellis swallowed. 'They said they thought they'd heard, well, *shots*, Staff. Gunshots . . . down at Alfa Zulu.'

16

Tallow blinked at him, remembering the negative answer from the gate, then hit the locking bar on the arms cabinet fast. 'Doing this must make me look some kind of nut,' he thought bitterly. 'I mean, hell, people just don't go shooting people in Scotland. Not *people*, they don't.'

But the sick spasm in his guts told him they did. Because he was an old soldier, and old soldiers have a feeling for these things. And he didn't want to go out there in the bleakness to be another of the people who got shot at, not when he had a nice cushy job lined up in the Corps of Commissionaires when he became plain Mister Tallow in three more months. And there were all the little Tallows, just waiting for Dad . . .

Yet he knew he was going to anyway, because he *was* a soldier. And because there were things in that grey building across the compound which shouldn't belong to any man but, if they had to exist in all their hideousness, then please God that they stay under British control.

So he swung round on Ellis and the other two men of the guard who'd just come in, slammed a full magazine into the Sterling submachine gun from the rack, and jerked his chin. 'Who's duty driver then?'

The cherubic faced one jumped. 'Er, me Staff.'

'You then. An' you, Thomson. Sterling and four mags each, on the double!' He turned to Ellis. 'Happen it's all a false alarm, lad, but you stay here by the door. If you hear anythin' that even sounds a bit like more gunfire then you get on that bloody phone to B.H.Q.

jaldi. Tell 'em Red Alert, they'll have everythin' from Custer's mob down in this area within . . .'

He hesitated, thinking what a bloody shoestring way to run an army, then smiled without much humour. '. . . within a week!'

He winked re-assuringly at the Cherub, switched the light off to prevent silhouetting in the open doorway, and ran crouching to the waiting Land-Rover. Neither of the two men who apprehensively followed him guessed at the sick clutch of fear that made Staff Sergeant Tallow want to stay curled up in that foetal, protected posture for ever.

*

Down at Alfa Zulu they were still waiting.

The man with the Czechoslovak rifle never lifted his eyes from where he had been expectantly gazing at a point on the skyline, just to the left of the Pill Box itself, but the girl found her attention kept wandering. She just couldn't ignore the reproachful gleam that seemed to reflect from Bulldozer's lovely boots, now upturned in the indignity of death.

She was glad when the leader finally looked at his watch again and, noting the climbing second hand, gave a curt order in a curiously harsh, unresonant tone. Instantly the ring of men around her jumped lithely to their feet and, with the precision of a well rehearsed drill movement, each turned inwards to face his neighbour almost as though forming for some strange, macabre reel among the corpses of the slain.

The leader swung to face her and, like the kid's boots, the canister strapped to his chest glinted dully in the Volkswagen lights. This time his eyes were hard and emotionless as he rapped out a second word of command. She was only conscious of the tremor in her hand as she raised it to the butterfly-winged turnswitch on the face of the canister and twisted it through a complete revolution. She wasn't really aware that, in the same instant, every man in the assault group had performed an identical operation with the equipment of his opposite number.

But she did know, because of all her previous hours of training for this mission, that she too now carried premeditated death between the warm swell of her breasts.

A third and final order. Silently the commando moved through the gates and, in infantry line of file, advanced under cover of the glare towards the Pill Box on the shoulder of Ben Dhearg.

Each man indifferently stepped across the body of Corporal Grey as he lay staring blankly at the sky. All except the girl and she, perhaps sub-consciously aware of her flared mini-skirt, stepped around him.

But Provost Corporal Grey didn't mind either way any more. He had now been dead for three minutes and twelve seconds precisely.

*

The Land-Rover hit an unexpected bump and Staff Sergeant Tallow only stayed in his seat through an experienced grab for the hand rail across the dash. Behind him he heard a resounding crash as Thomson's compo-soled boots returned abruptly to the alloy floor, then the butt of Thomson's Sterling caught him a painful graze under the ear and he glared angrily at the Cherub behind the wheel.

'Slow down f'r Chrissake!'

The Cherub looked even more nervous and hunched a little lower in his seat, but he still kept the speedo hovering on the forty mark because he reckoned that the faster they were going the less chance they had of being hit by any ambush.

Which shows just what an inexperienced young squaddie the Cherub was.

And then they were over the shoulder of the mountain and going like a bat out of hell down the twisting road past the Pill Box towards the glare from whatever had piled up at Alfa Zulu. Tallow strained to see behind the blinding light, at the same time viciously slamming the cocking handle of his submachine gun into the 'fire' position – right now it was a bloody sight better safeguard for all those little Tallows than a Prudential insurance policy.

They got to within eighty yards of the lights before Tallow dimly discerned the kneeling line of men beside the access road. Even while he was screaming 'Keep goin', lad! Right through the bastards!' he knew it was too late as he felt the Rover swing wildly under the drag of Cherub's panic-dictated brake foot.

By the time the crazily drifting Rover broadsided

past the ambush point – tyres screeching and smoking under the two ton, thirty mile an hour thrust – every weapon in the assault group was firing into it.

The centrifugal force of the skid counteracted the impact of the first twenty rounds to hit the rapidly dissolving Corporal Thomson, momentarily holding his body upright in the back of the vehicle. Then Thomson disintegrated at the same time as the windscreen, the Cherub's head – and Staff Tallow's dreams of retirement.

While the riddled quarter-tonner cartwheeled into the gate hut in a tumblingweed ball of fire, Tallow was projected at some three hundred feet per second into the inflexibly strong wire meshed grid of the fence.

The Staff Sergeant stayed alive just long enough to read N.O.S.H.E.B.'s prediction ... DO NOT PASS THIS POINT OR YOU MAY BE KILLED!

Which, he considered, was just as ridiculous as people shooting at people.

In Scotland!

*

From the duty room door Ellis heard the crackle of small arms fire and forgot all about being like Burt Lancaster.

It took him four minutes to realise the telephone cables had been cut outside the perimeter.

*

The three Provost lance-corporals in the Pill Box were

a lot more experienced than their once cherubic faced oppo.

The heavy M.G. opened up through the bracken covered aperture even while their detachment commander was still airborne, but the first deliberate burst passed well above the heads of the commando in a supersonic, whip-cracking canopy of tracer.

All seven men and the girl hugged the ground with the shock of being hopelessly exposed while, behind them on the road, the protective headlights snapped out as the heavy calibre shells dissected the Volkswagen's fore end with the efficiency of an acetylene flame.

When the gun on the mountain stopped barking the attackers knew that the gunner was only weighing up their disposition over open sights. He wasn't in any hurry, the targets were laid out like ducks in a shooting gallery below him, just like the sappers who built the Pill Box had intended.

God, yes he was scared bloody gutless at the idea of actually killing someone, but there was Staff Tallow to square up for. An' that doggy corporal with the one track mind. Jeeeeze, he must've bought it right at the bloody start, him and the other kid down there on the gate. Poor sods . . . ! That's it, mate. Snap the back sight down. See those two bastards squeezed in behind that clump of gorse . . . ? Traverse . . . traverse . . . Oh Christ, but I want to be sick . . . Finger round the trigger . . .

*

Lance-corporal Ellis started to run for the door of the big grey building across the compound, then skidded to a halt and scrambled back into the duty room to grab a Sterling and a couple of magazines. He tried to smack one into the rectangular housing on the side of the gun like he'd seen John Wayne do in hundreds of films, but the bloody rotten thing fell on the floor.

He was down on his hands and knees, sobbing in terrified frustration, when he heard the staccato smash of the Pill Box M.G. opening up for the second time.

He didn't stop searching for the lost mag, though. They put you on a charge if you lost a mag of live ammo . . .

*

The two commandos on the leader's right started to run crab-wise across the mountain, drawing fire away from the main group, as soon as the first clips of gorse showered down on them. He watched them go dispassionately, they were only gaining milli-seconds. Then the next burst from the Pill Box chased after the scrambling men, and overtook them, and they were rolling and tumbling in a welter of puppet's limbs and blood-soaked heather.

The machine gun rested again, confident in its tactical superiority.

Slow movement from the left and a sharp intake of breath from the girl. Someone was snaking his way, belly flat, towards a shallow depression running obliquely uphill to pass behind the hidden M.G. post.

23

And only one grenade through the aperture could tip the scales enough for some of them to make it over the crest ... the leader barked urgently until a haze of concrete chips hung over the hump of the Pill Box as a blanket of covering fire coned in from the intruders.

Unruffled, the M.G. smashed again from under its two foot thick umbrella, ploughing up the open ground between the main group and the gully. The crawling man seemed to half-roll to the lip of the depression, nearly to safety, then the girl was sobbing while the phosphor-red tracers vectored across towards him.

Until, abruptly, the machine gun stopped racketing with an impact of silence more shocking than the slam of a bullet.

But the man on the edge of the gully couldn't move either. They saw the threshing arms and the eyes white in the fear-suffused face as he struggled to free the canister strapped to his chest from the roots that entangled it. The harsh rasp of his breathing carried across the steady patter of the falling rain.

The left flank man started running to help, slipping and stumbling across the twenty yards of clumped, wet grass. Still the Pill Box stayed silent and menacing ...

... 'Charlie. Oh Jesus, Charlie! We gotta blurry jam ... get them fingers out the way f'r .... Oh God, there's one of them running across to the right, look ... an' some silly bastard stuck on the edge of that dip ... Right. A full mag now ... a fuggin' *mag* f'r Chrissake! ... Belt it in ... cocking handle back ...

finger on the trigger . . . Please God. Don't let it jam again. Not again. . . .

*

Lance-corporal Ellis found his lost magazine and felt a bit better. Thank your lucky stars you found it before Staff Tallow came back, boyo. So now what? Still go over to the big building? At least it's granite – granite protects you from bullets a bloody sight better than this wooden shack . . . But they're not firing out there anymore. Maybe Tallow's sorted out whatever needed sorting out. An' he didn't say to leave the duty room, did he? An' you don't like what they say about what's behind all that granite. I mean, you only went in there once when you was section runner, and all them shiny pipes an' test tubes an' glass shapes an' stuff – you got scared to hell, didn't you? And the blokes all dressed in white gear, with face masks an' little rubber boots like in that film with Karloff . . .

He decided to wait until Staff Tallow returned. A bit more of the weapons manual and a bit less of John Wayne saw the full magazine nicely seated in the Sterling just as the Pill Box started firing again.

*

The man hung up on the lip of the gully finally made it to cover – but only through the propellant energy of the first eight rounds to hit him. The second commando just kept right on running over the edge of the same depression and might have been perfectly all right if the ninth shell hadn't caught him square in the left side of his skull while still in mid-air, flipping him carelessly end over end and leaving him with legs jerking spasmodically towards the crying clouds.

The alien force was now reduced to fifty per cent of its original strength – and by a gun that should never have been allowed to fire.

But then the plan caught up with the schedule of attack, while the rain pattered steadily on the corpses of men who came from a country where it seldom rained at all.

The girl heard the sound first and raised her head, cautiously disbelieving. Beside her the leader tensed, eyes fixed on the point above the shoulder of Ben Dhearg. The girl's hand felt for his and squeezed nervously as, together, they watched the helicopter coming in from the south west, clawing urgently for height to clear the barren outcrops of the mountain.

It looked very frail against the tumbled sky, long insect body hanging almost incredibly beneath the circular blur of the rotors while, suspended between the landing skids, the watchers could see the reason for its lack of buoyancy – in the three black steel drums nestling untidily in the rope mesh of a cargo net.

The man hugged the Czech rifle and thought irrelevantly, 'A Sud Aviation Alouette.'

Then the machine gun, perhaps alarmed by the curious beating roar above it, started firing again in sporadic, searching bursts while the three remaining men and the girl dug their foreheads in the rough wet heather and clung to the face of the mountain. And prayed.

The helicopter skittered through a fifteen degree arc, black drums swinging crazily beneath, then it was hovering and roaring directly above the impregnable Pill Box with the bubbled Perspex canopy glinting like the swollen eyes of some great pillaging dragonfly and the downdraught from the rotors flattening the bracken all around the concrete post ... until the throbbing roar of its motors even drowned the now terrified smash of the Provost machine gun ...

... and the drums fell, while the unleashed Alouette soared vertically for a full, uncontrollable hundred feet with the pendulous sway of a storm-blown leaf.

The girl sensed she was screaming, though she couldn't hear anything but the roar of the napalm flames as they spewed over the Pill Box, seeking and finding every crevice and aperture. Then the blast came, carrying with it a tornado of flying gun-cut debris. And after the blast – the heat, a heat which shrivelled and bit into the fine hairs downing the hands of the four survivors while they clutched pressurised ears and grovelled even deeper into the now precious wetness of the mountain.

And then it was still, and very quiet, and the girl knew that the British soldiers were dead, had ceased to exist within their blackened concrete tomb, and she started dazedly to scramble to her feet, but the leader's arm cut the legs from under her and she fell again, sobbing with shock.

He blinked re-assuringly at her, then his arm crept round her shoulders and he held her down, close to the ground, until she found out why as the screeching tornado returned, but this time in reverse – driving and roaring with great, sucking breaths back into the huge vacuum left by the napalm flames, and only dying when the red oxygen glow turned to the matt black of an oily smoke cloud climbing vertically into the grey sky.

The man beside her waved briefly to the helicopter as it fussed uncertainly on the fringe of the pyre then, bending, he helped the girl to her feet. He smiled for the first time, white teeth showing strongly against the black grime, and slapped the butt of the model 58.

The four doubled up the road that ran over the shoulder of Ben Dhearg, towards the granite building lying undefended on the other side. The girl was the only one who looked back to where her compatriot's legs still projected, rigid in death, skywards over the lip of the gully.

She wondered numbly if the canister on the dead man's chest would be as effective, now that the body was lying in that inverted, undignified position.

*

Actually the target building wasn't completely undefended. Provost Lance-corporal Ellis was still guarding it.

He heard the helicopter roaring over the mountain and thought, 'Bloody good! They've reported the firing

28

from the village and Brigade's called in an air strike, maybe from R.N.A.S. Lossiemouth.'

Smiling a hard Kirk Douglas smile he ruggedly picked up the Sterling, threw open the duty room door – and absorbed the full force of the blast from the erupting Pill Box two hundred feet away!

Ellis took off backwards as far as the rear wall of the hut, slid to a sitting position among the glass shards on the floor and stared, eyes wide with shock and fear, at the volcano on Ben Dhearg. A smear of raw napalm flickered on his cheek, then died. Then flickered again and burst into a searing, vitriolic lance of flame. Ellis screamed in uncomprehending agony and, still clutching the Sterling, stumbled blindly towards the shattered door and the help that must surely lie behind the granite walls of that terrifying building.

'Oh Mother! Dear *God*, Mother. . . . They got white coats an' little rubber boots, haven't they . . . ? An' doctors wear white coats, don't they . . . ? Oh Jesus, it hurts. My face . . . it *hurts* . . . ! Mother. . . .'

He tumbled out into the smoke and rain just as Staff Tallow came running up. Ellis said 'Help me, Staff,' and started to cry. Then the running man fired from the hip and the first bullet took Ellis in the shoulder.

He spun round, sobbing he was sorry he lost that mag, Staff, but honest to Christ he'd found it again . . . then he realised that the man with the gun wasn't Staff Tallow at all and somehow, without any celluloid images to guide him, his finger found the trigger of the Sterling and it was bucking and tearing in his hands while the running man stopped running in blank surprise and went down to his hands and knees, jerking like a kitten's paper lure.

Then the man was face down and not moving at all, partly because he was dead and partly because the twenty eight rounds from Ellis's magazine were expended, while Ellis clutched at his shoulder and his burning face alternately and just hoped he'd done the right thing . . .

. . . until another man carrying a Czechoslovak automatic rifle ran up and shot Ellis three times in the chest right when he was shrugging apologetically like Henry Fonda, and saying he was sorry but the bloody thing went off by itself. . . .

*

The big double doors of the target building were formed from African mahogany, and locked. The acid-engraved plate screwed to them said, positively -

N.O.S.H.E.B.
KEEP OUT!

The leader looked over his watch at the remaining commando and the girl. They had very little time left, no time at all for a tactical entry. Glancing only briefly at the helicopter hovering almost solicitously above Ellis's body in the compound he beckoned to the girl to stand on one side of the doorway. Pressing back against the polished grey stone across from her he nodded slightly.

Straddle-legged, the other man fired a two second burst into the satin-nickel key plate and, kicking the splintered panels wide, went fast and low into the sterile green entrance hall beyond.

A glazed side door to the right opened and a white coated technician came out like a bolting rabbit. The man in the doorway snap-shot him and he slammed down with a screaming crash, skittering crazily across the shiny compo floor in a revolving starfish of snow white limbs.

The barrels of a twelve bore, which had probably been brought to Dhearg to shoot grouse – certainly not men – slid round the door frame and threw a terrified left and right into the already pivoting gunman.

It was only the reflex action of a blind finger which sent a stream of Russian short rounds pumping back through the thin plaster boarded partition wall.

The leader, sliding round the vulnerable corner, was just in time to see the second, and last, duty technician at Glen Dhearg High Tension Research Station tumble face down in a scatter of Ely Smokeless Cartridges, highly recommended for the Sporting Gentleman.

*

They had seven minutes left.

*

The helicopter settled in the compound five minutes,

thirty seconds later; just as the man and the girl came running back out of the big building. The man carried a black leather case with bright brass locks.

He carried it very carefully indeed.

Bending low under the flail of the rotors he jerked open the Alouette door and passed the black case up to the pilot who placed it, gently as a fall of swansdown, in the sorbo-rubber container behind him.

The girl was urgently tugging at the webbing release buckle below her breasts, nervously aware that the butterfly turnswitch on her canister had almost returned to the vertical as the timing mechanism whirred relentlessly.

It was time to go.

As the man started to slip his own device from his shoulders only the faintest trace of relief escaped through his eyes. He had earned the privilege of removing it. Earned it by staying alive and unwounded, because his orders stipulated that only the survivors could do this, and then only at the last minute when they were sure to evacuate the scene long before the outraged wrath of a raped British Army could arrive.

There was to be no evidence. No indication of the nationality or creed, or even colour, of the attackers. No pointers as to the origins of the commando which had ravaged Ben Dhearg. . . . The pilot of the helicopter gunned his motor impatiently as the leader scrambled into the tight space of the cabin beside the already waiting girl.

And then the man who had been blinded by a grouse

gun appeared at the doorway of the big building, and held his hands out imploringly towards the sound of the helicopter motors. And the canister still strapped to his chest glinted coldly as a splash of watery sunlight felt its way over the hulk of the mountain.

The girl bit her knuckles in horror while the man beside her tensed, remembering that the blind man had been his friend as well as a patriot. He arrested the pilot's hand before it touched the throttle then he was dropping down through the open door of the cabin until he knelt, hair plastered in wet black tentacles over his face by the beating, roaring downdraught of the rotors, and raised the Model 58 for the last time.

The burr walnut stock jumped against his shoulder as the blind man staggered tiredly down the steps and sat abruptly, almost gratefully, in the middle of the compound.

His finger squeezed the trigger again and he was clambering back into the Alouette even while his comrade fell over sideways to snuggle chummily into the body of Lance-corporal Ellis.

The black napalm cloud, hanging like an oily shroud over the Pill Box, shredded into long farewell streamers when the helicopter cut through it and slid behind the shoulder of Ben Dhearg.

The glen seemed very quiet after it had gone.

*

The butterfly turnswitch on the canister around the blind man's chest clicked into the vertical position.

Followed by the one on the inverted man in the gully. And on the two huddled untidily on the muddy slope near the riddled gorse bush. And on all the corpses of the others who had helped to kill Provost Corporal Grey and Staff Tallow, and poor bloody Ellis, and . . .

. . . and, suddenly, there were no men left at all. Only bright cones of fire where once they had been, as the canisters hissed through the chemical changes activated within them, then dissolved in a spreading, devouring phosphorous of destruction.

And even the flames were gone by the time the first belated patrol of Jocks bumped grimly down the long, empty road through Glen Dhearg.

A Plague of Sailors

Chapter One

Chief Officers have the dubious advantage of giving orders without actually having to do the manual work. That's why I nodded to the cadet to secure the docking phone and, leaving Chippie to screw up the windlass, slid down the ladder from the foc'slehead for the last time on voyage number fifteen of the good ship *British Commander.*

Skirting the bosun's gang, already removing the wedges from number one hatch cover, I threw a gloomy eye over the dripping panorama of warehouse roofs surrounding the dock. London looked wet as it usually did at the end of a trip. Bloody wet and bloody miserable. Not at all like Haifa, our last port of call. But Haifa was Israel, and it was always sunny in Israel, sunny and pretty as you approached it from seaward with the low coastline shimmering and dancing in the Mediterranean glare . . .

. . . until you got close enough to make out the red dust-cloud still hanging over the Promised Land three days after the earthquake.

Rain. A hanging, endless mist of rain. A steady haze varnishing everything in sight, pockmarking the oil-scummed surface of King George the Fifth Dock while the flotsam collected sullenly under the rubbing strakes of the lighters as the tugs chaperoned them in to *Commander*'s outboard side. I hesitated at the rail under the break of the centrecastle and looked down on the floating corpse of a dead dog I could have sworn was there when we left, outward bound, four months ago. Lighting a Capstan Full I flicked the discarded match out in a spiralling curve, watching as it drifted to settle beside the drum-tight, distended cadaver below.

Rain. And corpses. The poor bloody Israelis may be queueing at the Wailing Wall to pray for the former — if there was any Wall left — but by God they had plenty of corpses now. Twenty thousand under the imploded discothèques and plush hotels of Tel Aviv alone was the first estimate. And another twenty, maybe thirty thousand, entombed on a half moon arc between Caesarea and the Dead Sea while they still tried to fight their way through earth slips and fissures to re-establish a land corridor into the Holy City.

The dead dog bumped almost plaintively against the scarred anti-fouling below. Corpses. And disease. Only the rescue squads and disinfection teams were allowed into Tel Aviv now while three thousand troops ringed the city to ensure the New Death didn't spread.

The rats had appeared on the second day, scurrying and squeaking in the baking, red-filtered sun. Burrowing and squirming into places where only the unlucky people were still alive. And rats have fleas. And fleas are the parasites which spread disease. And disease thrives on the imprisoned corruption which forms an earthquake's heritage. Bubonic plague, typhus, dysentery, rabies ... so no one went in, or out, of swinging Tel Aviv any more.

A Ford Transit van drew up alongside the gangway and the driver ran nimbly aboard, dodging past the duty quartermaster as he slipped the silver-painted stanchions into their sockets and started to reeve the guard ropes.

A large poster stared at me, sad and appealing, from the side of the van, a little black kid with enormously wise eyes and a pathetically ballooned stomach. The British Red Cross were chartering part of our outward space, along with Oxfam and half a dozen other relief organisations. Needless to say the Jewish League had a fifteen hundred ton consignment waiting in the transit sheds while the U.S. Army, with typical over-kill generosity, were shipping over the earthmoving plant from their Surrey-based 82nd Engineer Regiment to back up the 79th already flown out by Hercules transports.

The blown-up dog nodded cynically at me, galvanised into a ghoulish bobbing by the wash of a passing Customs' launch. I blew a streamer of smoke back and smiled bitterly. Every cloud etc. ... funny how even the worst disasters always seemed to spawn some good. A new San Francisco from the ashes of the old. Tighter safety regulations at sea as a memorial to the fifteen hundred dead of the *Titanic* – and now the first glimmerings of peace between the Arabs and the Jews.

At this moment, two thousand miles away, Israeli

paratroopers were digging shoulder to shoulder with Arab Legionnaires. Black bearded and ringletted Orthodox Jews from the Hebrew University on Mount Scopus divined for the trapped Muslim bazaar keepers of the Suq al Attarin... ' Shalom! Peace, Mahmoud... !'

Hussein had been the first of the Arab statesmen to offer help, tentatively perhaps, even when his own Jordan was reeling from the overspill of the tremors. Then the other neighbours. Blankets and tents flying in from the Lebanon, plasma and D.D.T. from the Syrian Arab Republic. They'd sent shovels and quicklime too. How was that for macabre common sense?

Or, maybe, just wishful thinking?

Even Sadat was a Good Samaritan-elect, with his much publicised gift of a shipload of Canadian grain purchased at the express order of the Egyptian Presidency Council and now loading in Montreal en route for Haifa and a great big backslapping let's-forget-the-Six-Day-War-and-be-neighbourly ceremony. Still, a magnanimous gesture from a president who had a million near-starving Fellahin of his own to cope with.

Unless, of course, the new friendly U.A.R. man's policy of Love, not War was slightly influenced by the Israeli guns and tanks squatting stolidly as ever along the stagnating Suez Canal. And the fact that one of the first post-cataclysmic operations carried out by the Jewish sappers was to repair the convulsed runways of their strategic fighter bases, still allowing the sleek Mirages with the Star of David decals to scramble for the Gaza Strip the moment they were needed.

But then, I have a nasty, cynical way of assessing things anyway.

I spun my Capstan butt to join the match and the passed-away Fido. Either way it didn't matter much to the little Haifa kid I'd seen with only the dust-caked head and big black eyes protruding from the rubble of his home, who whispered 'Papa, Papa,' over and over again – then died just as Papa dug Mama out to find she didn't have any head left at all.

The line of yellow bulldozers crouched patiently along the wharf, waiting their turn to be swung aboard and chocked down as deck cargo. I wondered which one of them would be used to cleave a new Dizengoff Street through the ruins of Tel Aviv. Or prepare a new foundation for a second Mandelbaum Gate. Or even search for the enormous stone under the Dome of the Rock from which Mohammed leapt to heaven on a horse, David constructed his altar, and Abraham sacrificed Isaac.

Or maybe just to lay a carpet of yellow quicklime for the massed graves they were said to be excavating between the parading lines of olive trees in the Garden of Gethsemane.

I shivered and climbed the ladders to the boat deck, just as the first Red Cross bale swung aboard.

*

McReadie was waiting for me in my cabin when I went below. As I went in he was flopped back on my bunk with his feet up on the chest of drawers looking for all the world like a carbon copy of a 'sailorman at home'. Mind you, he had the decency to remove them the moment he saw me glowering irritably.

'J.C. wants to see you, Mister Mate,' he grinned. 'About ten minutes ago.'

Then he swung his bloody legs up on to my chest of drawers again.

McReadie was my conscience. Like Jiminy Cricket was with Pinnochio. Except it was me with the wooden head in this case. He was also the British Mutual Steam Navigation Company's operations superintendent.

Which – on consideration – was a very odd post to be held by a serving commander in the Royal Navy.

But then, we were all very odd people in B.M.S.N.C.

*

It must have been around the time we'd first picked up the Lizard Light that a little boy called David Soutar found some old oil drums near a flooded gravel pit on the route between Kirkcaldy and the Forth Road Bridge. He made a splendid raft and launched it with all the childish gravity of a seven-year-old embarking on the Great Adventure.

David drowned nine minutes later.

The Fife County Constabulary frogman who recovered David's body also found what felt like a car under the pea-green waters of the quarry. The Kirkcaldy Fire Brigade registered considerable surprise when, on winching it ashore, the large metal object turned out to be a helicopter.

A Sud Aviation Alouette helicopter at that.

*

McReadie had one of those ostentatious James Bond-type dragsters that was all chrome-plated wheel spokes, dentist chair seats and four and a half litre engine. While I don't think he could actually blast his oppo through the roof at the flick of a switch the impression you got as a passenger was that it would happen anyway, just as soon as he hit something.

He forcibly strapped me down, screamed 'All systems go, go, gooooo . . .', then the 'G' forces rubbered my face out of shape as we took off down K.G.V. wharf like a horizontal Apollo Eleven behind schedule. I just screwed my eyes tight and wished to Christ they'd sent a raving lunatic in a rocket sled to collect me instead.

Then I remembered J.C. wanted to see me in a hurry, which made the possibility of a Metropolitan traffic holocaust a perfectly acceptable risk.

Because J.C. was A Big Man.

Oh, not so much in stature perhaps, as in personality. That's why those who knew him referred to him as 'J.C.' When you first met him his eyes held you far more than the slightly limpid grip of his handshake, while the aura of authority he exuded made you want to call him 'Sir' even when you weren't a naval officer and he didn't have the trappings of a holy stoned quarter-deck and a nervously fussing flag lieutenant as a backdrop.

J.C.? Actually the initials had a vaguely familiar ring to them in another context but, once you'd met him, J.C. would always mean James Cromer – or Vice-Admiral Sir James Cromer, V.C., K.C.M.G. when you were looking him up in Burke's. Or in the Who's Who of Big Business.

Or – as a result of his pre-retirement capacity as something rather sinister in the Admiralty – when you browsed through the files of the American C.I.A., or the Soviet K.G.B. Or even the Ta Chung-Hua Jen-Min Kung-Ho Kuo Bureau of Counter Espionage. . . . They all said J.C. was A Big Man too.

They also knew that, as Chairman, J.C. currently had an absorbing interest in the affairs of the British Mutual Steam Navigation Company of London. In fact, that he'd launched into retirement in 1961 by virtually prising the financially foundering company from the Receiver's hands and, with uncompromising efficiency, had re-built it into a reasonably profitable and expanding shipping line with nine dry cargo carriers in service and two more under construction.

But they *weren't* aware that the six million pounds sterling bolstering up the capital structure of the reconstituted B.M.S.N.C. had been discreetly provided by Her Britannic Majesty's Government – through several unimpeachable nominees, of course – and they certainly didn't know that the Company's ships were very much more sophisticated and adaptable than any average, ordinary cargo boat would ever need to be.

Or that all B.M.S.N.C. crewmen were British

Nationals hand-picked, ruthlessly trained and in-doctrinated, and turned out of a very unconventional mould.

Like me – Brevet Cable.

*

By the time we arrived in the basement garage of B.M.S.N.C.'s head office in Leadenhall Street the corner of my left eye had developed an uncontrollable twitch. The high speed Otis lift that took us through fifteen of the sixteen floors to J.C.'s penthouse opera-tions suite did much the same for a nervous tic at the corner of my mouth. When McReadie finally steered me out into the reception area I was running through the gamut of facial expressions usually associated with a Kamikaze second pilot after an aborted mission.

But it was on the fifteenth floor that they really separated the men from the boys.

Nobody, but nobody, could ever make it up the narrow entrance to the sixteenth unless J.C. wanted them to. And only then after they'd been screened, identified, and given clearance by the two coldly polite mock Corps of Commissionaire men who greeted you at the lift. At least it made B.M.S.N.C. a head office with a touch of originality – it was the only shipping company building in the world where a gate-crashing super-salesman would get an unarguably final 'No'. With a nine millimetre bullet, if a more polite refusal wasn't enough!

I mean that the British Mutual Steam Navigation

A Plague of Sailors

Company was a front for one of the most audacious confidence tricks in the history of espionage. An overt maritime commando with free access to every port in the world where trade with Britain was necessary – and it was no coincidence that, every time British interests were threatened abroad, the Lion Passant house flag of B.M.S.N.C. fluttered discreetly alongside that aggressor's discharging wharves.

Like when the *British Venture* off-loaded machine parts in Odessa during the Cuban Crisis, or when the *British Regiment* filled her 'tween decks with animal hides from Nanking while Mao was putting the squeeze on Hong Kong – The thermo-nuclear devices welded into their number eight double bottom tanks would have provided an interesting ace up our sleeve if diplomacy had failed to win the game.

Not that it was all big bangs and fall-out with us in B.M.S.N.C. For instance, there was that strange case of the Polish trawler fleet mother ship which struck what was presumed to be an old W.W.2 sea mine in the approaches to Gdansk. The Reds never did salvage the information she had stored in her electronic analysis computers about our N.A.T.O. ultra-sonic code frequencies ... and *British Commander* had cleared the Gulf of Danzig well over an hour before.

Or the choking deaths of one hundred and twenty three crewmen of the submarine *Sovetskogo Soyuza* when she inexplicably sank less than three miles off Cape Wrath after successfully surveying our potential northern convoy assembly anchorages ... and there wasn't a Royal Naval vessel within fifty miles, just a casually passing merchantman called the *British Allegiance*.

Her *Ikara* A/S missile launcher was transhipped to a curious R.F.A. armament support ship long before she off-loaded the rest of her deck cargo in Glasgow.

As McReadie once said: 'Once upon a time when we wanted to give 'em the message we'd anchor a brace of cruisers offshore, polish up the guns bloody lovely, and throw a cocktail party for the civic brass. Then the local wogs would take one look and say, "By the great toe of Allah, only a mighty nation could produce such warships as those. We must give up our evil ways and follow the red, white and blue path of righteousness".

'Now when we show the flag they just pour petrol over the bastard an' burn it ... if we had a cruiser available in the first place!

'So, instead, we send you scruffy sods in under cover of the Red Duster as a sort of poor man's naval presence – and not only do you create a lot more havoc with a lot less publicity ... but you show a bloody *profit* as well.'

But that was just because McReadie was a passed-over Commander R.N. doing penance for his sins as the B.M.S.N.C./Ministry of Defence liaison officer or, as he succinctly put it, 'The run-around kid for a flock of Joseph Conrads with spy cloaks and bloody football bombs!'

McReadie presented me to the sergeant commissionaire behind the desk with the air of a sheriff bringing in a fugitive. 'Mister Brevet Cable, mate of *British Commander*. For Chairman's briefing.'

Sergeant fixed me with a baleful, suspicious glare. 'Yessir. Your I.D. code . . . Sir?'

I swallowed nervously. McReadie went in and out all the time on the strength of his regular pass, but sea-going personnel were away for months at a time and required more careful identification on their return. And J.C.'s security screen were an independent élite, McReadie's presence wouldn't sway them from violent inclinations one bit if they thought I was an impostor.

'Juliet x-ray wun fower zero . . . echo,' I said, tentatively precise.

Sergeant blinked at me disappointedly for a moment, then swivelled round to rummage through a card index on the reception desk, searching with a frown of intense concentration, his lips forming the sequence J–X–1–4–0–E.

Finally he conjured up a photostat identity card from which a series of pictures leered Neanderthally back at him. Side, face and full length, and all indisputably of Brevet Cable.

Despite my nervousness I felt a twinge of self-approval. Tall? – A skin of paint under six foot. Ugly? – Never! Well, just a little bit . . . but sexily attractive with it. Debonair? – So who could look debonair in a merchant navy uniform . . . ? Still, it did give me that salty, bucko mate and mean with it look that appealed to the more masochistic nymphomaniac. And the three rings on my cuff added a touch of authority which made station porters and snack bar attendants jump like their trade unions had suddenly ceased trading.

No one else, mind. Just station porters and snack bar attendants. Sergeant looked even more disappointed and picked up the red internal phone before him. 'Commander McReadie and Mister Cable, Sir. For briefing.'

He nodded at the phone, then the steel door behind him slid open noiselessly. The chamber we entered was brilliantly lit and bare. Anyone inside it was as exposed as a fly on a white Formica table – and it wasn't just newspapers they used to swat you with. I motioned to the row of brass nozzles just visible in the far wall while McReadie smiled like the smile on the face of the tiger.

'BZ Anti-riot Gas,' he said enthusiastically, 'courtesy of the U.S. Army. Bloody marvellous as a harassing agent. One inhalation causes dry flushed skin, slowing of physical and mental activity, urinary retention, tachycardia, constipation, giddiness and disorientation, maniacal behaviour, increase in body temp . . . !'

'F'r Chrissake, McReadie! So you've got your medical diploma,' I cut in irritably, 'So how long does it take for the poor bastard to recover from it?'

He looked hurt. 'Quite a long time, really . . .' he answered, as if explaining to a child, '. . . seeing we'd have to shoot them anyway if they ever made it this far.'

*

At the next stage I was met by a beautifully dressed

49

blond young chap wearing a buttonhole carnation and a disapproving expression.

He said, 'Is your name Cable?' and I said, 'Oh Jesus, not *again*?', then J.C.'s voice bellowed, 'Don't arse about, Ballantyne. Get them in here!'

Ballantyne stopped staring suspiciously and looked petulant instead. My lips were framing the conventional, 'I must protest, Sir . . .' when I entered J.C.'s briefing room, but his counter-attack was a text-book illustration of one-upmanship. '*Commander* was nearly twelve hours behind her E.T.A., Cable. What kept you?'

I could have said an earthquake. But I didn't, partly because J.C. scared the hell out of me and partly because irrelevant Acts of God like typhoons, plagues and cataclysms weren't allowed to disrupt B.M.S.N.C. schedules anyway. Instead I fixed my eyes stolidly on a point three inches above his head and looked suitably chastened. The little admiral surveyed me calculatingly for a moment, then leaned forward, pushing something towards me across the desk.

I looked blankly at the scrap of mottled, slate-grey sponge suspended in the liquid-filled glass vial under my nose.

'You ever seen a bit of a man before, Cable?' he said with the pride of a virtuoso collector. 'I mean, for instance, a piece of a human lung . . . ?'

*

Twenty minutes later I still didn't know exactly what I was being briefed for, and I didn't have an explanation of the Frankensteinian exhibit in the alcohol bath – but I'd learnt quite a lot about the curious happening that had occurred three days previously, before *Commander* had berthed, in a place called Glen Dhearg.

I found it hard to believe, though. I mean, people just don't go shooting at people. Not in Scotland.

Then McReadie produced some colour prints of a bullet-riddled and burnt-out Land-Rover, and I could see that the desiccated corpse half shredded through the steel meshed fence beside it had been a Military Police staff sergeant at one time. And another poor sod with half his face corroded with napalm and a gunshot wound instead of a chest, he'd been a brown job too.

And the three, maybe four, shrivelled black monkey-sized cadavers huddled round a skeletal machine gun within a carbonised concrete tomb . . . I suddenly started believing everything they told me about Glen Dhearg.

I wondered who in God's name would want to do a thing like this. They must have left some leads to follow up. J.C. answered my unspoken query with Kodacolor-X's to make a selection of horror film stills look like a sneak preview of Bambi. This time the mini-corpses were even smaller, each one within its own five foot radius of super-heated ground, melted and deformed beyond belief – and each little black doll could once have been an Englishman.

Or a Chinaman. Or a Hindustani. Or a South American pigmy.

'Phosphorous,' McReadie said, 'All of them must

have carried a phosphorous incendiary, probably either remote controlled or time actuated. A sort of do-it-yourself cremation kit. They tried to make sure we wouldn't trace the dear departed for a long, long time.'

'*Tried* to make sure?' I asked.

J.C. nodded at the little bottle with the sliver of lung tissue. 'One of them was shot sitting down . . .'

Behind me McReadie murmured, 'Lazy bastard,' but I didn't turn round.

'. . . He fell against the body of one of our own men. The redcap absorbed a lot of the thermal output from the incendiary and that much undamaged tissue was recovered from the attacker's chest cavity by the Home Office pathologists.'

I tried not to look as squeamish as I felt. 'You mean you can establish the origin of the attackers from . . . that?'

'No. But we do know that one of them was between twenty-five and thirty years old.'

'Ah,' I said, 'That narrows the field quite a bit then.'

'We also have one rather more specific lead,' McReadie broke in smoothly, 'Forensic examination shows that the tissue sample came from a heavy smoker. The lungs were heavily adulterated with nicotine tar.'

I smiled sourly. 'At least you've proved smoking can kill.'

'When I want a bloody comic instead of a chief officer I'll get a proper funny one, Cable.' J.C. levered himself to the vertical and looked superior. 'Analysis of the tar content has provided one interesting piece of information . . . it contains an alkaloid substance found only in tobaccos blended by a firm called Abbas Hedayat Company of Damietta.'

'Damietta?'

'Egypt. West of Port Said.'

I shrugged. 'I smoke Virginian, Sir. It doesn't mean I wear a stetson and whistle "Dixie".'

J.C. permitted himself a withered imitation of a smile. 'The Abbas Hedayat Company don't export, Cable. Their output is strictly for consumption within the U.A.R., in fact largely within the immediate area of the Nile Delta. If you've ever tried a real Egyptian cigarette you'll appreciate it's an . . . ah . . . acquired taste.'

I knew what he meant. Like pickled walnuts and matured yak dung. Which, I had to admit, made the chances pretty reasonable that at least one of the visitors to Glen Dhearg was either an Egyptian national or someone having had a long residence in the Land of the Sphinx.

'What about the bomb that was used to phase out the Provost M.G. post?' I asked. 'Bombs have to come from somewhere.'

McReadie shrugged. 'Drums of napalm dropped from a great height. The Yanks use the technique a lot in Vietnam to flush out the Viet Cong warrens. We'll trace them eventually, or Special Branch will anyway, but a forged consignment note can turn a drum of napalm into a drum of motor oil at the stroke of a ballpoint.'

'And the helicopter?'

'It's been found.'

'So find the owner of the Alouette and you've solved the problem,' I suggested deprecatingly, 'Helicopters are traceable . . . Sir!'

J.C. glanced at me sideways, like a python sizing up a suckling pig. 'We've already found him, Cable. Two days ago. His name was Alistair McKay, ran a small ariel survey business from Edinburgh Turnhouse.'

I spread my hands, it was like teaching your Grannie to suck eggs. 'Interrogate him and you'll get a lead to somewhere. Even if he was on solo charter he could tell you who was using the chopper.'

'He probably would at that, Cable,' J.C. murmured mockingly, 'if his passenger hadn't pushed him out of the machine two thousand feet above the Tay Estuary.'

Which stopped me being so bloody clever but still didn't answer one question which still nagged me – just where did B.M.S.N.C. fit into all this? I mean, we were J.C.'s private armada of *seagoing* trouble shooters, and ships don't sail particularly well over Scottish mountains. And anyway, the only thing you can steal from an electricity board is electricity, which hardly constituted a threat to the security of the State.

But J.C.'s telepathic mind beat me to the draw as usual. 'You will receive a more detailed briefing along with McReadie when you go next door, Cable, but I should emphasise the gravity of this matter. Every counter-espionage department, not only Special Branch,

has been directed to make maximum effort to recover
what was taken from Dhearg. That means us too.
You'll be going back to Haifa with *Commander* as
originally planned . . . what was your original mission?'

He knew perfectly well, but maybe even Pontius
Pilate liked to be prompted by Iscariot occasionally.
I shrugged. 'Nose around the disaster areas, assess their
emergency service capability in the context of a phased
nuclear attack . . . and, on the way in and out of Haifa
Roads, carry out an underwater electronic survey to
check whether the quake has upset our previous
soundings. In case we ever want to send in a midget
submarine probe.'

J.C. nodded. 'They could become an embarrassment,
the Israelis . . .' I didn't say anything but it struck me
then that another planner had said something similar
about forty years before. He'd died a bit later, in a
Berlin bunker. The Admiral gave up his political
speculation and came back to the present, '. . . you'll
have other investigations to make while you're there
now, Cable. McReadie will instruct you . . . My
compliments to Captain Caird aboard *Commander*!'

I blinked at McReadie who jerked his head towards
the door. The interview was over and J.C.'s head was
already bent over the next file of papers for attention.
The Great Man had spoken, the administrative trivia
was left to the peasants.

Hesitating at the door I turned back resolutely.
There was one detail I felt J.C. ought to explain
himself. He glanced up impatiently as I spoke. 'A small

point, Sir, but ... what *was* taken from the Hydro Board that was so vital?'

He frowned. 'Hydro Board?'

I matched him frown for frown. Two could play at being bloody-minded and obtuse. 'Glen Dhearg. . . . The High Tension Research place.'

He looked like a man who was dealing with an idiot. 'High Tension nothing, Cable. Dhearg was only a front for the limited production of C.B.W. agents . . .' He smiled wintrily, '. . . B.M.S.N.C. aren't the only phonies around.'

I didn't smile back because I couldn't understand the joke. 'C.B.W.?' I queried tentatively.

'Chemical and bacteriological warfare, man.' J.C. jerked his head irritably, 'I thought McReadie had told you that much. But whoever attacked Glen Dhearg took enough bacilli with them to kill every man, woman and child in the U.K. twice over. You may be familiar with the name, Cable, if not with the results . . .'

I ignored McReadie tugging at my sleeve as I felt the first spasm of horror digging into my belly. J.C.'s eyes were very cold and hard above the little bottle containing a piece of a man.

'. . . it turns your blood black, Cable. They call it anthrax!'

*

In the adjoining office McReadie looked at me severely when I said, rather stupidly, 'Anthrax is for cows, dammit. It's a bloody animal's disease.'

'And your English is bloody atrocious too, Cable,' he murmured irrelevantly. I noticed, though, that the casual flippancy didn't reflect as far as his eyes.

On the other side of the table the cadaverous Ministry of Defence C.B.W. man shook his head. 'The anthrax bacillus is generally obtained from animals affected by splenic fever, yes, Mister Cable. It can, however, be transmitted to man either orally or externally and was, in fact, known a number of years ago as "wool-sorters" or "rag-pickers" disease due to its frequency among workers of that description.'

He smiled. A dried-up, humourless little smile to match his text book dialogue. 'Or you can refer to it as "malignant pustule", if you have a penchant for colourful description.'

McReadie produced the inevitable snapshot. This time the print was in black and white but it didn't stop me averting my eyes from the mass of streaming, gangrenous sores on the thing under the camera lens.

'Oh my dear Christ!' I muttered, thinking that it could never have been an ordinary man, not like McReadie or myself, yet at the same time knowing it had. I wondered how long it had been since the unspeakable monstrosity had originally contracted the disease.

I also wondered about the circumstances under which the photograph had been so conveniently taken, but I didn't ask. You don't. Not in our private little world.

The C.B.W. man tapped the print with a long,

delicate forefinger. 'A victim of Anthrax-B will approximate this condition within twelve hours of contamination, gentlemen. Death will occur inside a further six . . .' He hesitated, then continued in an almost apologetic tone, '. . . I'm afraid this only shows the primary stages in the development of the disease, the carbuncular phase. The terminal process involves, literally, a general dissolution of the body tissues. It's not . . . ah . . . not very nice, is it?'

An understatement to which the only adequately British answer I could offer was a strangled, 'No.'

'Anthrax-*B*, Professor?' McReadie queried almost conversationally. But then, he'd known about the hideousness on Ben Dhearg a lot longer than I had.

'The form of bacillus stolen from Scotland, Commander. My contemporaries there were most successful in developing this rather more virulent extract which was, at the same time, completely sophisticated and controllable . . .'

'Controllable?' McReadie and I echoed together.

'. . . controllable in that contamination can only take place by oral means . . . ah . . . adulteration of the enemy water supplies. Infusion of the bacilli extract into foodstuffs, medicines. . . .'

McReadie leaned forward and said, very deliberately: 'You're an enthusiastic, wicked old bastard aren't you, Professor? You and all your long-haired crowd of mates. You make Adolf Hitler sound like the saviour of the world. God only help us if the other side have any like you.'

The C.B.W. man took off his glasses and polished them vigorously. Replacing them he looked at McReadie with enormously solemn, unblinking eyes. 'Ah, but they do, Commander,' he murmured softly. 'I can most earnestly assure you, they do.'

And I suddenly started to wonder how many hours after infection it would be before the agony of my hydrating blood cells drove me out of my mind. Because I knew then that it could happen. But the tough, bucko mate image in me finally struggled to the surface and I gave a good imitation of an impassively cynical shrug.

'Only a fool goes to war, McReadie,' I said brutally, 'but it's a bigger bloody fool who goes to war without a weapon as big as the next bloke's. Anyway, we're pretty nasty people ourselves in B.M.S.N.C. We're one pot who can't afford to call the kettle black for starters.'

I finished with an ineffectual, 'Apart from which, we're *British*, dammit! We'd never really use the bloody stuff.' Then I sat down feeling like a cross between Colonel Bogey saluting the Colours and the man on the end of the Thin Red Line.

But the Professor just had to go and undermine my logical re-assurance. His face crinkled into the faintest suspicion of a smile. 'I'm sorry to disillusion you, Mister Cable, but . . . we already have.'

I glared at him irritably, '*I'm* talking about germ warfare.'

'And so am I. About the first and, so far the only,

recorded case of a bacteriological weapon being employed as a strategic expediency. And we were the nation responsible.'

Beside me McReadie laughed disbelievingly but the C.B.W. man continued with academic detachment. 'It is a matter of historical record, gentlemen, that in 1763 during the Pontiac Conspiracy, the then Commander-in-Chief of the British Forces made a ceremonial gift of smallpox-infected blankets to two rather ... ah ... recalcitrant Indian chiefs. I would suggest that the ensuing lack of opposition considerably expedited the westward expansion of the colonists.'

I wasn't impressed. For one thing they didn't have the alternative of the more socially respectable genocidal machines two hundred years ago. Like thermo-nuclear cannons. 'You said "the only recorded case", Professor. But didn't the Americans allegedly use B.W. in Korea? And what about the late Nasser's gallant aviators in the Yemen? Now, those were boys you could have been *really* proud of.'

He shrugged, he was bloody fire-proof. 'There was no foundation for the charges made against the United States Forces in Korea. That was a propaganda weapon, Mister Cable, not a bacteriological one. And in 1966 the Egyptians employed chemical – not "B" weapons – against the Yemeni tribesmen. Phosgene and mustard gas ... painful but far less fatal.'

'Why anthrax?' McReadie cut in grimly. 'Or this Anthrax-B as you call it?'

A gleam of fervent interest showed in the Professor's

eye. He became as precise as a computer and suddenly we were talking to an insulated, scientific mind, not to a human being with human feelings.

'We must really give some credit to the United States Army Chemical Corps at Fort Detrick for this decision. For several years they have been experimenting with all the potential B.W. agents. They've found that many diseases were worth consideration, and were sufficiently adaptable. . . . The rickettsial diseases, such as Q-fever. The viral diseases – dengue fever, ence-phalitis, psittacosis . . . parrot fever, y'know? . . . coccidioidomycosis. And then, of course, the bacterial diseases . . .'

'Of course,' I muttered, reeling under the deadpan monologue of horror.

'. . . Dysentery, brucellosis, pneumonic plague, tula-remia. . . . Now take tularemia, gentlemen – laymen's cognomen, rabbit fever. Rather a gentle "B" agent in that, while the infection potential is almost one hundred per cent, the actual mortality expectation may be as low as only thirty per cent of the population, even if untrea. . . .'

'Why *anthrax*?' McReadie's voice was very tight and low. But maybe he didn't use the same yardstick for gentleness as the Professor.

The cadaverous features looked slightly disappointed, like a man interrupted in mid-hobby. 'Because anthrax remains viable and extremely virulent throughout the breeding phase, storage, transportation to, and delivery on, target. It disseminates successfully and, most vital, does not decay too quickly in the field. . . . You understand, gentlemen?'

'And this . . . this "B" bacillus?' I ventured dully, 'Apart from having a purely oral application, what other *advantages* does it have over the good old fashioned, unsophisticated cow's disease?'

The Professor inspected us over his glasses. 'I suggested earlier that one of the virtues of anthrax is that it does not decay too quickly in the field. Perhaps this was somewhat of an under-statement. One of the very few field trials of B.W. agents during the last war was the spraying of the island of Gruinard – off the Scottish coast – with anthrax germs. The experiment had little practical value other than to illustrate that the unfettered anthrax bacillus is practically indestructible in its natural domestic form. Gruinard is still uninhabitable, and will remain so for the next hundred years.'

He polished his glasses again and looked rather pleased. 'Our new strain – the Anthrax-B bacillus – retains a life cycle, when activated, of only four to five days depending on the ambient temperature. Add a further forty-eight hour safety factor and an invading army can move into the target area without even the necessity for large scale injections of anti-anthrax Sclavo serum. . . .'

He replaced his glasses and leaned forward towards us. '. . . Gentlemen. In Glen Dhearg we have produced the Ultimate in sophisticated weaponry!'

McReadie didn't clap. Not even once. 'In Glen Dhearg,' he said softly, 'you have produced a screaming nightmare beyond the vision of an Edgar Allen Poe. You have produced a horror which may shortly turn this England into a rotting, leprous desert of lifeless corruption. . . . Congratulations, Professor.'

I shook my head to clear the web of fear paralysing my mind. I knew now what my primary mission in Haifa was to be. It was the same as every British agent all over the world – to search, and pry, and spy until every trace of Anthrax-B was either recovered or destroyed.

But how do you find an object the size of a Thermos flask that could kill a hundred million people?

Until the hundred million people had died. . . .

Then the blond Ballantyne slammed hurriedly into the room, looking viciously pleased. 'You'd better get back down to K.G. Five, Cable . . .' he sniggered.

'. . . Your ship – *British Commander* – she's on fire!'

Chapter Two

I would have preferred to rush back to the ship in my own safe but sure way – on the bus – only McReadie insisted on my company in his custom-built bullet again. And this time he was really in a hurry. Strangely, the only conscious memory I have of that crazy ride was a deep feeling of relief that I was at least returning to a world I could understand and cope with.

The revelations of mass-homicide and over-kill horror awaiting a push button burst of national superiority had left me sick and empty inside. I was a professional seaman, with the sailor's love for the uncomplicated, semi-monastic environment of a ship at sea. Oh, admittedly I was also a trained and dedicated member of J.C.'s ocean-going band of patriotic thugs yet, even in that, there was something clean and wholesome and exciting – a reflection of the spirit of Frobisher and Drake. Of brooms at the masthead, death to the French, and singe the King of Spain's beard.

So maybe McReadie and myself and the rest of the B.M.S.N.C. crowd *were* two hundred years out of date with our skull and crossbone bloody awkwardness and our unfashionable conviction that the British were still great even if Britain wasn't – but we were both cost-effective and discreet with our little bits of cold war mayhem.

And if the hot war ever came we'd still go on sailing the ships – only we'd die a lot more often doing it – because then the subterfuge would be over, and the Red Duster would become a target instead of a cover. But even that would be nice, just for a bit, to see the old lion on the house flag get up and growl a little without being afraid anyone might hear . . .

. . . then McReadie prodded me and said, 'We're here,' and I opened my eyes to see the high flare of *Commander*'s bows above me, with the crazy paving network of white firehoses breaking up the wetness of the wharf around her.

I jumped out and overtook McReadie at the bottom of the gangway, noting as I did so that the canvas threadlines hung in pulsating loops abeam of number two forward hold. I visualised the cargo stowage plan for our recently completed homeward leg. What the hell had been awaiting unloading in number two . . . ? Oh Jesus – rubber! Bales of rubber loaded in Port Swettenham and consigned for Haifa . . . but when we got to Haifa they didn't have any docks left to unload it so we came on to London to trade it for bulldozers and blood plasma instead.

Rubber! Which meant that, if the fire had a good seat down in *Commander*'s guts she could keep on burning for days, burning until it ate the bottom right out of her and they either towed her off to sink in deep water or she settled in the mud and filth of K.G.V. to await the even more destructive flames of the breakers' torches.

I went up the accommodation ladder three steps at a time.

The second mate, Dave Ball, met me at the top. He looked like a sailorman made up as a burnt-cork imitation of Al Jolson. 'Whereaway?' I yelled.

'Number two upper 'tween decks! The Old Man and the Chief are down there now with the Firemaster.'

I skidded to a halt, subconsciously noting the tear in his sleeve and the mottled patches of firefoam staining the front of his uniform. '*Upper* 'tween decks? You sure, Two Oh?'

He nodded, then doubled over in a paroxysm of coughing and spluttering. Straightening up he grinned wryly. 'Bloody smoke. Sorry . . . Yeah, we were lucky this time. It started in a single line of bales stowed inboard of that late Penang consignment. Ingot tin, remember? They must have insulated the rest of the hold, prevented it from getting a good grip. We lost, maybe, a couple of dozen rubbers an' a lot of sweat.'

I felt the relief buoying me up. I remembered the tin. I also remembered cursing the last-minute shippers, too. Chief Officers don't like heavy cargo stowed high, it knocks the hell out of your stability calculations. But this time God must have been standing right astern of me when I accepted the shipment even though we'd actually closed for cargo much earlier.

In fact, I was so damned glad to still have a berth

I didn't think too deeply about *why* the rubber had decided to burn. At least, not right then.

McReadie was right behind me as I moved forr'ad, stepping over piles of half-charred dunnage and limpid cargo matting. Two firemen came past at a jog-trot, vaguely alien in their swept-back helmets and shiny black thigh boots. I noticed the sweat streaks on the soot-encrusted features and the stark whiteness of the eyes where the smoke goggles had protected the skin, giving them the tired image of a racing driver on his lap of honour.

Except that nobody ever gave them a laurel wreath and a champagne-filled trophy when they won their particular race against time.

Sliding down the forward centrecastle ladder to the well deck I glanced outboard at the wharf and the red ring of firetenders surrounding the ship. 'They were quick,' I shouted to McReadie over my shoulder, 'Bloody quick!'

A steel meshed cargo net trailing little whisps of floating, smoking latex swung over our heads and out on to the wharf where helmeted troglodytes from the blue-flashing armada below sprayed the simmering bales into dank submission.

Clambering over the steel coaming of number two I climbed cautiously down the vertical ladder to where Captain Caird stood talking grimly to our chief engineer and a fireman with a white helmet and boot polish face. The Old Man swung round as McReadie and I approached.

'So you're back, Mister,' he growled, making it obvious by his tone that he disapproved of his chief officer playing war games while his ship melted down to the waterline.

'Yessir!' I shuffled guiltily, almost as if he'd caught me with a can of paraffin and a candle.

'What happened, Captain?' McReadie asked, completely unruffled. But then, he was one of the bosses anyway, and he didn't have to live with the Old Man all the time.

Elliot, the Chief, stepped forward and angrily kicked at a smoking slab of hatch cover. 'Bloody sabotage, Mister!' He spat to clear the stench of burnt rubber from his mouth, 'A bastard firebug. That's what happened.'

McReadie glanced at me while inwardly I groaned. As if we didn't have enough problems with the Dhearg cock-up already crowding hard on our heels. He frowned. 'You certain, Chief? This lot couldn't have been ignited very long before it was discovered. Wouldn't an arson attempt be made while there was no one around? Give it a chance to get a good grip?'

The Old Man shrugged and I caught the gleam of perspiration varnishing the craggy forehead. 'It was, Commander. Only we were lucky it stopped raining before he expected it to.'

'Raining?'

'Aye. The stevedores had only been in the hold long enough to offload the hatch square itself, then it started to rain again. They rigged the tent awning and buggered off under the break of the foc'sle for a smoke. And that's when the fire must have been started.'

Caird smiled briefly through the worried creases. 'I'm not much on religion, McReadie, but I could have sworn that rain had set in for the day. Anyway, the dock gang didn't hardly have time to light up before the weather cleared and the tent came back off. Then they saw the fire.'

I closed my eyes and breathed deeply. It was the wrong thing to do. By the time I'd stopped coughing the sun was sliding behind the grey clouds again and another shower started to patter dismally into the already saturated mess of number two hold. I was almost sure, though, when I looked up, that the watery, vanishing orb bloody winked at me.

I rubbed my stinging eyes. 'That still doesn't mean sabotage, Sir. I mean, there's spontaneous combustion. Or even some silly bastard sneaking a fly smoko in the 'tween decks. . . .'

The Firemaster shook his head and held out an object. 'You ever seen anything like this, Sir?'

I had, but only in scrapyards. To me the thing was unrecognisable as anything but a lump of twisted, semi-molten metal. I raised an inquiring eyebrow and he grinned. 'No, probably not. But we see a lot of them, too bloody many for that matter. It's been a butane torch, sort of a portable blowlamp. They're handy things to have around the house for little solderin' jobs and that . . . and they burn damn' hot for, maybe, thirty minutes on an eight-bob cylinder. It's long enough to start quite a nasty reason for callin' us in.'

'And that was found . . . ?'

'Over there. Between the two bales at the centre of the outbreak. Presumably the incendiarist hadn't known about the rest of that side being non-inflam material, otherwise. . . .'

I knew what he meant. Only the early removal of the hatch tent coupled with the firebug's ignorance had saved *Commander* this time. But why? Why the hell should anyone want to sabotage the ship? Could it be someone hitting back at B.M.S.N.C.? Someone like the Russians? Or even the Chinese? Was our cover finally blown . . . ? No! Foreign powers supplied saboteur's tools infinitely more sophisticated than an eight-shilling blowlamp. And anyway, if the Kremlin had found out about our crowd they'd use a much more effective method of cancelling us out — like a homing torpedo up our hawse pipe one anonymously dark and windy Atlantic night. . . .

Then McReadie said, 'I want every man in that stevedore gang questioned. By Special Branch.'

The Old Man added viciously, 'And I want them all bloody castrat . . .'

But with shocking unexpectedness *Commander*'s siren started shrieking hysterically from the great funnel above us, and the invisible fire pumps on the quayside suddenly revved into a crescendo of activity.

While a dull, booming explosion astern made the steel plates under our feet shiver in agony . . .

And the Second Mate stuck his head over the line of the hatch coaming and screamed, 'Jesus, but we're on fire again! We got another bloody fire aft . . . !'

*

I remember seeing the Chief snatch his oil-stained uniform cap off in disgust, kicking it skitteringly into the wet filth behind me, then McReadie said imperturbably, 'It's all go, isn't it?' and started running for the ladder.

I felt someone's boot sole crush agonisingly on the back of my hand as I went up, but the second explosion cut me off in mid-yell.

Topside everything was confusion until you realised that our own crewmen were moving forward in disciplined groups to allow the firefighters free access to whatever was burning aft. Unfortunately, at the crest of the tidal wave of men in the alleyways, little knots of dockers and wharfies rather spoilt the manoeuvre by not knowing whether they should be doubling forward, aft, or straight up in the bloody air.

And, somewhere in that maelstrom of cursing bodies, was the still very active firebug!

I grabbed Dave Ball's arm. 'Where the . . . ?'

The Second Mate looked white and shaken. I noticed the firefoam streaks on his reefer now had an overcoating of oil. 'Bosun's store. After end of the centrecastle . . . Jesus, Brevet, it was bloody horrible. They'd just come back aboard to start working the after hatches. We were opening up number four when someone yelled "Fire" and I looked round to see smoke jetting from the contactor house ventilators ... I un-dogged the door, then Micky Stern came charging up with an extinguisher. The silly bastard went in before I could stop him, then ... then something must've blown. Christ, Micky came out backwards along with all the loose gear. Pulley blocks, paint brushes an' scrapers, buckets ...'

He shook his head but I let him go on talking in that shocked, mechanical way. There were plenty of people better qualified to handle the outbreak and Ball had to talk himself out to someone.

'... he was screaming, Brev. We just couldn't stop him screaming!'

I bit my lip. 'How bad? How badly was he burnt?'

He shook his head again. 'I don't know. Two of the firemen tackled him, rolled him in an asbestos blanket. I doubled forr'ad to raise the alarm. He was still ... still on fire when I left.'

The funnel stopped blowing and I glanced up at the bridge front just as the fourth mate, Packard, stuck his head over the rolled-down dodger. 'Second Engineer's been on the phone from down below, Sir. Says he's worried about the contactor circuits being shorted out if they're using water. He wants to shut down the generators.'

I waved irritably. 'How the hell do I know what's happening at the other end of the ship, Packard? Tell him to belay everything till I get word to him. I'm going aft now.'

The Fourth waved stiffly back with all the injured dignity of a brand new gold stripe on his arm and disappeared into the wheelhouse to his muster station at the communications panel. High in the sky above *Commander's* monkey island a mushroom of oily smoke diffused into the grey rain. I realised that I was soaking wet and that my collar was gradually mutating to a pulpy choker, and started to feel miserable as hell. My favourite pipe-dream of becoming a farmer suddenly struck me as well worth earnest consideration.

Jerking my head at the second mate I climbed the ladder towards the activity at the head of the gangway. Out on the wharf an urgency of bells indicated the arrival of an ambulance and I saw the crowd of grand-standing longshoremen press forward in buzzing expectation. Forcing my way through the surge of bodies I turned back to Ball.

'Take charge here, Two Oh. For Pete's sake try and get some sort of one way system going – forward traffic down the starboard side, aft movers up the port alleyways.' I was slowly finding out that fires and accidents meant a lot more than being pretty sharp with a hose jet and a bucket of sand.

The scene round number four hatch was like something from a Hollywood war-at-sea film. Bits and pieces of ship's gear littered the deck, spewed from the Bosun's store by the exploding drums of oil. Smears of red, viscous liquid dripped sullenly from the surrounding bulkheads and, for a terrifying moment, I felt I'd

73

entered a set-piece of incredible carnage. Then I realised the blood was just anti-fouling sprayed from super-heated drums inside the steel oven, and I relaxed slightly.

Until someone shouted 'Move it!' and I saw what was on the stretcher between the two St. John's men.

They hadn't been able to cover Micky Stern with a blanket after they'd finally extinguished him, he was too badly burnt. I didn't know whether he was already dead or whether they'd given him a shot of morphine, either way he didn't move as he passed. I couldn't help staring with the ghoulish fascination of a luckier man, but what lolled on the canvas litter made me remember, with shocking impact, the monkey men of Glen Dhearg and the dreadfulness of the Damoclean threat called Anthrax-B.

Suddenly I wanted the firebug very badly indeed.

And I could see, as I stepped over to where McReadie stood, that he did too.

'They're going in now,' he murmured, watching as a smoke-helmeted section officer moved carefully into the charred blackness of the store. Whispy bubbles of high expansion foam floated in the heat turbulence behind him as he glided waist deep like a subterranean monster in a bubble bath. Another Brigade man had slumped on the steel deckplates between two of his mates, retching painfully through a soot-bordered hole of a mouth, and I thought being a fireman was a bloody awful job too.

Another two men waded into the steel cocoon and, a moment later, handfuls of charred debris were being thrown out while a high pressure jet swept some of the filth into the scuppers. The Firemaster came over and, removing his helmet gratefully, wiped his face with the back of his sleeve. The protected white band below his hairline made it look as though he had a two-tone lid to his skull.

He scratched his head vigorously, 'There's someone doesn't like you, Captain.'

The Old Man shook his head fretfully. 'Why us? There's a lot of ships in this dock. Why us, dammit?'

I said, 'How much damage this time?'

The Firemaster shrugged. 'Not too bad . . . you lost a lot of gear in there mind. And the electrical systems on the other side of the bulkhead'll need checking out. We've got a man in there now, keeping an eye open. Otherwise, you've been dead lucky again.'

The Chief snorted like an angry bull. 'Lucky! Like hell we've been lucky. Christ, it's like tellin' a bloody ex-virgin she was lucky goin' out with a rapist instead've a homicidal maniac.'

I cooled the simmering Chief down by feeding him the second engineer's problem, noticing out of the corner of my eye that the fourth mate had slipped down from the bridge and was having a discreet word with the Old Man. The Captain's eyebrows met in a ferocious 'vee' and he shook his head violently. 'I'm damned if you will, Mister Packard. Not phone them yet, you won't.'

He signalled to McReadie and myself while the Firemaster walked away and the Chief evacuated, muttering, to his beloved engine-room. The Captain watched as we approached, then suddenly seemed to find the foremasthead of absorbing interest. 'The master of a vessel owned by this Company often finds himself in the peculiar position of having to overlook certain ... ah ... extra-curricular duties carried out by his subordinates. Am I correct, Commander McReadie?'

McReadie grinned surreptitiously at the way the Old Man was picking his words. 'Quite correct, Captain Caird.'

'Mmmmmm. Then it would be most wrong of me, would it not, to precipitate any further such actions by revealing that – in precisely thirty minutes from now – I intend to advise the dock police that Mister Ball has detained in the saloon ...'

McReadie and I were already moving for the ladder.

'... a man who, he has reason to believe, may be the incendiarist?'

*

The firebug-elect was only a kid really.

Two of *Commander*'s larger able seamen moved aside from the door of the saloon to allow us passage, then drifted shoulder to shoulder again like concrete-filled blockships. This was a B.M.S.N.C. problem and no one else was invited.

Except for the long-haired, eczema-faced youth

76

flanked by Second Officer Ball and Bosun Clegg, of course.

He was scared sick, you could see that by the way his eyes kept darting wildly round the saloon. He didn't look particularly guilty, though. Not like a bloke who'd just burned all the skin off a man. When he saw me he was noisy too, and cheeky with it.

'Hey you, Captain bloody Bligh! You tell these fuggin' yobbos ter keep their bloody 'ands to themselves or I'll ... !' But we never did find out the alternative because the Bosun wrapped a hand like a dustbin lid round the kid's face and he stopped doing anything for a few minutes, including breathing.

Ball said, 'The Bosun noticed him hanging round the after end of number four just before the fire started, Sir. I've already asked the ganger about it and he says the lad wasn't in his squad. I checked and it turns out he was originally working in number two. Where the first blaze started.'

The Bosun removed his hand and the kid sort of collapsed into himself and started to cry. The Second Mate's evidence wasn't exactly conclusive but I thought about how Micky Stern's wife was going to be crying too, and stepped forward. 'Have you searched him, Mister?'

Ball nodded at a small pile of articles on the table. There wasn't much, just a grubby hankie, a few bob in change, a bunch of house keys. And a box of Swan Vestas.

I picked the matchbox up and sniffed. It stank of

paraffin. And there had been paraffin in the Bosun's store, several drums of it. I rattled the box under the youth's nose and grated, 'I don't want to know your name. I don't want to know your private bloody history, or the ages of your mother, girl friend or dog ... But I *do* want to know why you bloody did it.'

'Did what?'

'Lit the fires!'

'I didn't!'

I grabbed him by the collar and shook him until his head wobbled dangerously. We had about twenty-one minutes left before the police arrived, and they weren't as nasty as we were. There were too many of the Company's ships at sea to risk not warning them in time if the B.M.S.N.C. gaff was finally blown.

I yelled close to his ear, 'I didn't ask you *if* you did it, ratbag ... I asked you *why* you bloody did it!'

The kid started yelling hysterically, 'I didn't! I didn't ... Oh my God, I didn't do what you said ... Please. Please Sir, I didn't ...'

Someone gripped my shoulder and I turned my head to see McReadie looking concerned. I blinked in sheer surprise and stopped trying to shake the lad's skull right off the end of his neck.

McReadie said anxiously, 'Easy, Cable, easy! Look, maybe the boy didn't do it. We need more evidence ... detain him, yes. But only until he can be taken into proper custody ...'

He smiled re-assuringly at the lad, '... you won't

get pushed around aboard this ship, son. The police will question you, but only within the limits of the law.'

The lad sniffed and wiped his eyes, trying to look tough again. 'I didn't do what he said – light them fires – so your big fat mate there can get hisself knotted!'

McReadie laughed weakly and I stared at him in shocked disbelief. So that's what happened when the Navy took charge. The gentlemanly turning the other cheek. The let's be terribly fair and British, and to hell with the thousand sailormen who may be sailing into the sights of a Soviet attack periscope this very minute.

And, to cap it all, that desk-bound, nine carat gold plated R.N. bastard was actually laughing at *me* aboard my own ship. And coming the chummy with a vicious little cretin of a firebug. . . .

I couldn't believe it, but I knew I was finished with J.C. and all his rotten crowd of bootlicking hypocrites. Men like McReadie there, who sent us out in ten thousand ton tramp steamers to attempt the work of cruisers, but didn't have the guts to face a five pound fine for assaulting a young thug who'd probably just burned one of his own men to death.

I saw the second mate and the bosun looking white and grim and knew they felt the same way. Then McReadie even started to tug the kid's jacket back into place and I felt the rage building up inside me. The bond of forced intimacy between them was so strong it made me want to get outside, out into the fresh, clean air.

I was about to spin abruptly on my heel and walk out of the saloon when McReadie raised an interested eyebrow and held the youth's lapel badge between finger and thumb. The incongruity of his next remark made me hesitate briefly. 'So Hitler's alive and well, and living in Knightsbridge, eh son?'

The kid shrugged cautiously, 'Maybe. I dunno. So what's it to you, then?'

Behind them the second mate frowned uncomprehendingly, while Bosun Clegg looked as if he'd like to spit all over McReadie. The Commander just grinned confidentially, 'You'd be surprised ... hey son, who's your section leader?'

'Alfie Ba ...' The kid's eyes narrowed suspiciously, 'Look mate, it's not illegal, but we don't talk about it either.'

''Course not. But you've got the right ideas, boy. Wish I had more time ...' McReadie fumbled in his pockets while I watched angrily, hating him as much for the small talk as for the counterfeit interest he was showing in the young thug.

But that was the Navy for you. They called it 'Keeping your own yardarm clear ...'

I thought, 'To hell with you, McReadie,' and moved towards him. I had fourteen minutes left and my last act as a B.M.S.N.C. man was to arrange for the bloody Commander to be sat on by the Bosun's brawny duo while Chief Officer Cable had an intimate *tête-à-tête* with Spotty Face. I could see that Bose and Dave Ball were considering a similarly independent move anyway.

McReadie hauled a packet of Senior Service from his Moss Bros tweeds and said casually to the kid, 'Smoke?'

The kid shook his head. 'No, ta, mate. Don't touch 'em.'

Which appeared to irritate Our Man In London somewhat.

Because McReadie hit the kid hard across the face and, grabbing him by the lapels in true bucko mate fashion, started to slam the back of the long hair against the saloon bulkhead in a most ungentlemanly way.

And yelled in a foghorn, quarterdeck voice, 'Then why the fuggin' hell are you carrying a box of matches, you little Nazi bastard? C'mon . . . Achtung! Achtung! . . . It was to burn this goddamned ship, wasn't it? I said, *wasn't* it . . . ? And I want an answer, pig's offal, before I cave your homicidal little skull right bloody in . . . !'

But then, I always said the Navy were all right.

*

'United Kingdom National Socialist League,' McReadie said cheerfully as we headed back at an almost safe speed to Leadenhall Street. 'Neo-Nazis, most of 'em. Hate Jews, spades, dagos, wogs . . . and your grannie's cat. But they especially hate the Jews. That's why he burned *Commander.*'

I forced myself to watch as we took a one way street the other way. 'And all to stop a few tons of aid getting to a place where people are dying by inches for want of it.'

McReadie smiled without humour. 'That's what's upset them, Cable boy. They're dying too bloody slow for that little yobbo's mob to wait . . . it was the badge that gave him away, ostentatious little bugger.'

'D'you reckon it was an official attempt? That the Party backed him up? Special Branch could have their guts.'

'Maybe. We'll never know for sure. Personally I don't think so. They're great on the hate propaganda but they don't do much about it. And anyway, the men at the top would have had more savvy . . . at least waited till the ship was loaded with outward cargo. But that's not really the point now. The important thing is that maybe, just maybe, that anti-Semitic thug has done us a great big favour . . .'

I swivelled round in astonishment. If firing *British Commander* had been a favour, for sinking the Q.E.2 he should get a knighthood! McReadie broadsided into Oxford Street in true amber-gambler style.

'Because I think, Mister Mate . . .' he murmured thoughtfully, '. . . he's told us exactly where to look for Anthrax-B.'

*

'M.O.D. think you need a long rest, Commander,' J.C. said pithily. 'They suggest the Retired List may be appropriate?'

I grinned surreptitiously. McReadie was as good as off my back, and I had a rider to add to the first maxim of Service life. Never volunteer – not even a theory!

And certainly not one as implausible as McReadie had just propounded. Even I knew that.

Then J.C. exposed himself as a man of deep deceit. 'I pointed out, however, that one of my most experienced chief officers also appeared to concur with your assessment. . . .'

When I realised he meant me I started to protest, 'I never sai . . . !' but J.C. rolled right on over me. '. . . The Ministry somewhat reluctantly agreed to leave the final decision in my hands. We may take independent action under our normal terms of mandate.'

Which was a neat way of bringing the bottom of the ladder into carrying the can too. And Brevet Cable's feet stood firmly on the lowest rung.

Then we went over all the 'why's' and 'wherefore's' and 'maybe's' again, and considered the added information made available to us by an intelligence network already stretched to screaming point but still covering more and more ground to trace the flask that could kill one hundred million people somewhere – anywhere – in the world.

Perhaps the dying had already started?

Apart from agreeing that – judging by the adulteration of the piece of human lung known as Exhibit 'A' – Messrs. Abbas Hedayat Company of Damietta should be investigated by their local public health department – we also made our first assumption.

That the attackers of Dhearg were of Middle Eastern origin.

J.C. said 'Probably Arabic?' but I just shrugged an indifferent acknowledgement because, even at this early stage, I felt we were pursuing a theory without a logical foundation. In fact, one half of my brain was already composing a letter of explanation to touch the M.O.D.'s heartstrings.

'So who do the Arabs hate the most?' McReadie had said, as we struggled with every permutation of our few scraps of information. 'Apart from each other?'

'The Israelis, I suppose.' I stared at him, 'You mean they might hit them with the Anthra ... You're off your bloody head, Commander!'

'Am I?'

'Yeah! Look, the Arab States are pushing a lot of aid into Israel just now. I mean, hell, they're *helping* the Jews. You don't kill a man by giving him a drink of water?'

'Or even a bar of soap, maybe?'

'Soap?'

McReadie spread his hands. 'The Jews have been helped before, Cable. Like when a few million of them came in from a long train ride and someone said "Take a shower, friend, you'll feel better". Except that when the little kids and the old men turned on the hot water all they heard was the hiss of cyanide gas. ... It happened in a place called Buchenwald, remember?'

'Beware the Greeks who come bearing gifts. Or, in context, should I say "the Arabs"?' J.C. examined the little bottle speculatively. 'It could give us both a motive, and a precedent.'

I shook my head violently. It wasn't good enough. 'Sadat wouldn't. Don't go falling into the national habit of assuming, because he's anti-Western, he's a natural monster. And Hussein certainly wouldn't.'

McReadie grinned sardonically, 'Why? Because he was educated in jolly old England, John Bull?'

'No. Just because he's a human being!'

J.C. waved the bottle and the little grey scrap swirled sluggishly. 'Then he already has something in common with the men who hold Anthrax-B.'

He stood up abruptly. 'Oh, stop being a complete bloody fool, Cable. Men – anonymous men – died to obtain this weapon . . . I said *weapon*, Mister! And they stole it because they have only one conceivable use for it . . . as an offensive instrument!'

'There are passive weapons too, Sir. Defensive ones.'

'D'you really think the British Government are going to admit publicly to having sanctioned the manufacture of B-agents after the Porton Down affair a year or two back? When they emphasised, even then, that we'd never produce more than the minimal quantities necessary for defence research? And remember – a weapon's existence has to be proved to the rest of the world before it becomes a deterrent. You only qualify as a nuclear power after making a bloody great, instrument-shaking bang. Whoever took this weapon did so because they needed it to attack somebody else.'

I made one last attempt at finding the fly in the logical ointment. 'All right. Assuming one of the Arab powers intends to use it – say the U.A.R. for argument. How could Sadat possibly justify its strategic employment against Israel? It would be like sending out open invitations for the Third World War, dammit.'

'He's already justified the use of phosgene and mustard gas. That's hard fact . . .' The little Admiral shrugged. 'Sadat's still a frightened man, with or without Soviet aid. And unless the Russians are prepared to dive into the Middle Eastern conflict right up to their necks – meaning total committal – then it's an even chance the Israelis could stomp both him and the Egyptian Presidential Council right into the ground if they wanted, even now. There are a lot of hawks in the Israeli Government just waiting to do that. *And* it may not be too long before Israel goes into the air with a nuclear capability . . .'

He smiled grimly. '. . . I'm a sailor, not a politician. But if I was convinced I had it coming one day in the near future – from the Israelis – I think I'd pursue a policy of genocide now and worry about what the Russians and Western Powers did to me later. And to each other. Anyway, Cable, nations don't necessarily go to wars of extinction over other people's principles in this enlightened age. The Reds would probably give it three censored lines in *Pravda* while the U.S. Government would rattle a horrified nuclear sabre, send Cairo a very strong note of protest ... and go back to wondering how to get right out of Vietnam so nobody notices. And you can't imagine we're going to make a fuss about it? We'll be far too busy covering our tracks and pretending somebody else had made the wicked weapon!'

I still thought he was being an optimist but to him the death of a few million Israelis and Arabs was of a lot less imminent concern than the disintegration of our National jolly-good-chaps-and-let's-play-the-game image.

To emphasise it, he shrugged. 'But, either way, it still doesn't neutralise the main issue – the fact that the British Government have sanctioned the surreptitious manufacture of B-weapons despite all denials. It would finish us as a stabilising influence in world affairs, turn us into international pariahs – Maybe even lead to our exclusion from the North Atlantic Treaty defence plan ... So either we recover Anthrax-B, Cable, or we're damned in the eyes of the world!'

Which meant that, if J.C. and McReadie were right, then all we had to do was search every square inch of Egypt, Syria, the Lebanon and, for good measure, Jordan. Then everything would be O.K. ... If they didn't actually happen to *use* the bloody stuff for the next two hundred years while we looked!

*

I was just deciding that maybe it wasn't such a good idea to go back to Haifa at this particular stage when I remembered something McReadie had said down in the car.

'Earlier, Commander, you were talking about how that Nazi firebug made you think the Jews could be the potential target in the first place. You also said "...He's told us *exactly* where to look for Anthrax-B".'

McReadie nodded and opened the intelligence file he'd collected before we settled down for the big fight. 'The info to date certainly bears out my original guess...'

I didn't say anything but I couldn't have thought of a better description for it myself. He leafed through a wad of Provost C.I.B. reports on the Dhearg massacre then pulled out another buff foolscap. '... the helicopter found at Kirkcaldy belonged to an Edinburgh firm, right?'

I nodded as he continued, with J.C. watching speculatively. 'I checked with the Immigration and Alien's Department of the Scottish Office. They need more time to check but ...' he looked pleased, '... we now know that three students were missing from their classes at Edinburgh University since Thursday last – the day *before* the attack on Dhearg.'

I must have appeared extra unimpressed for he looked at me calculatingly, 'Their names, Cable, were – Nazem al Qotar, age 24, Syrian national; Ghaleb Agha, age 26, also a Syrian national; and Anwar Abuzeid

Soliman, age 23, youngest son of Staff Colonel Kamal
Aziz Soliman, Egyptian Army!'

Suddenly I became interested.

McReadie continued, 'Al Qotar gives us another
slight lead in that he was believed to be a qualified
helicopter pilot. He was also studying to become a
geologist – his old man's something big in the U.A.R.'s
nationalised oil set-up. And geologists have a cast-iron
reason for chartering survey choppers. Incidentally,
the ground staff at Turnhouse can't remember any
thing other than that the man taken up by the late
Alistair McKay was young, dark and slim. But it could
fit.'

'It's not much,' I muttered doggedly, 'Three kids
don't make an army.'

'There's more. Like the chief officer of an Egyptian
freighter called the *Farafra* who went ashore in Dundee
on that same Thursday night and never returned
aboard.'

I looked disgusted. 'You might have told me all this
before. You said her chief officer?'

McReadie nodded. 'Name of Hosni. Aged about
thirty-five to forty. We're trying to get more on him
but there seems a possibility he was originally an
Egyptian naval officer. Peculiar, yes?'

'We're all bloody peculiar,' I said gloomily. 'All first
mates. It's the job. And you still haven't told me where
we look for the hot germs.'

McReadie got up and walked over to the wall map
of the United Kingdom hanging behind J.C.'s desk.

He stabbed with his finger. 'The Alouette was found here. Presumably the stuff was aboard her when she landed, before they ditched her in the quarry. So where would they go next?'

'As far away from our security net as possible?'

'I think so too. Which means abroad. How?'

'By plane. It's the fastest way.'

'It's also the most closely watched. The anthrax is in a largish container, don't forget. And the only way out of an airport is through Customs. It's too dicey.'

'So?'

McReadie scratched his head and looked at J.C. 'How else would you smuggle an article into a foreign country, Sir?'

J.C. plucked his lip thoughtfully. 'By ship. Slip it over the side before the rummagers come aboard. Into, say, a pilot cutter. Or a P.A. launch.'

McReadie nodded. 'My feeling too, Sir.'

I brightened. 'The Gyppo in Dundee? It's the obvious one.'

'I don't think so. If Hosni's involved then he wouldn't risk drawing attention to himself and her by jumping ship. And I checked, she sailed coastwise in ballast, straight down to Hull to load general.' He grinned broadly, 'Either way she's now being dismantled rivet by bloody rivet by specialists who even *look* like Customs men following up a narcotics tip-off.'

The Admiral said, 'What else sailed deep sea, ex-Dundee within, say, forty-eight hours of the Dhearg affair?'

'Just two Indian State Liners. Jute boats, Sir. But I have another idea.'

'I thought you might,' I murmured nastily.

McReadie stabbed the map again. 'Glen Dhearg to ... the Forth Road Bridge where the chopper was ditched. They were in a hurry. Would they overshoot Dundee like that, by forty odd miles? Or would they have a car waiting to hustle them across the Forth to somewhere nearer ... ?'

I jerked my chin. 'Like Leith?'

He looked pleasantly surprised to find I had a mind at all. 'Like Leith, Cable boy!'

The paper rustled again. 'There were four sailings from Port of Leith, Sir, excluding coastal traffic. All within two days of the hit ... a Clan Liner to South Africa; a Ben boat outward for Yokohama; a Frenchman with general for Toulon and ...'

He watched us closely. '... a Canadian passenger-cargo ship – the *Attawapiskat River*. Twelve passengers, one under the name of Fathi al-Rana'i; female Jordanian, age 22, destination ... Quebec.'

I noticed J.C. give an involuntary start but, apart from the Jordanian tie-up, I was still unimpressed. 'So?' I muttered blankly.

McReadie spoke very softly indeed. 'Quebec, Mister, is only a spit from the Port of Halifax ... Where a Liberian freighter is loading right down to her marks with grain this very minute. And bulk grain is the perfect target for Anthrax-B.'

He leaned forward. 'And this particular grain is –
I coin a recently used phrase – a *ceremonial* gift,
Cable. . .'

I started to feel sick again. '. . . from U.A.R.
President Anwar Sadat. To the citizens in the Republic
of Israel.'

Chapter Three

And that was the reason why – eleven days later – I found myself approaching the Straits of Gibraltar at a rollicking seventeen knots with the loom of the Cap St. Vincent Light punctuating the dark shadow of the coastline on our port quarter.

But I wasn't Chief Officer Brevet Cable, mate of the B.M.S.N.C.'s *British Commander* any more. I was just plain B. Cable Esq., stateroom passenger aboard a Liberian registered freighter called the *Ayacucho City* – and the U.K. passport I'd exchanged for my seaman's discharge book said I was an accredited observer of the International Seismological Society, en route to Haifa.

Which made me an earthquake expert.

On paper.

It also made me a very frightened man. Because, stowed in the six holds of the *Ayacucho City* below me, were eight thousand tons of golden grain from the big wheat country – enough to make the black eyes of all the little, starving children of Israel grow big and round and happy . . .

. . . until, maybe twelve hours after the feast, it turned the blood black in their veins while their bodies dissolved under the assault of a hideous biological mutation called Anthrax-B.

Maybe?
I still had to find out!

*

'She's the *Ayacucho City*,' McReadie had said. '9045
tons, port of registry, Monrovia.'

'Owners?' I queried.

'Greek firm – it's a flag of convenience set-up – called
Manentis Shipping. Payanotis Manentis is their chairman.' McReadie's face looked grimly rueful, 'Manentis
is a Jew.'

J.C. muttered 'Bugger it!' while I wore my usual
slow expression and looked blank. 'That's bad, then?'

'It's the worst, Mister. With some owners we may
have had a slim chance of approaching them discreetly,
checking out the ship and crew, but Manentis . . .' The
Admiral slammed the table viciously, '. . . He's one of
the hawks, Cable. Hates the Arabs as much as he did
Hitler. One breath to him of what we suspect and every
tank engine along the Suez could be roaring bloody
retribution. And the Russians won't allow it. They
can't afford to allow it. . . .'

'Anyone for nuclear tennis?' McReadie murmured
behind me.

I frowned. 'Presumably Sadat used a Zionist-
owned ship as part of the gesture, to create more
confidence. But it proves one thing – it's unlikely that
the *Ayacucho City*'s crew are involved, which means
we're looking for sabotage from an outside party.'

'Like the girl, al-Rana'i.' J.C. drummed on the blotter, 'The Liberian'll have some passenger accommodation, McReadie. Check her list through our Quebec office.'

'Looks like a United Nations problem,' I suggested tentatively, 'unless we have a few discreet words in Sadat's ear. Tell him the gaff's blown and please can we have our disease back?'

'You're a tolerable officer, Cable, but you'd make a bloody arse of playing diplomat!' The Admiral proffered the little bottle again. 'One scrap of a man's guts isn't proof, Mister. Anyway, even if we were certain, d'you really think the Israelis would sit back and let U.N.O. act for them with their usual effete hand-smacking? And the Egyptian Government? All we'd get there would be two-fingersful of self-righteous bloody indignation . . .'

He shook his head decisively, '. . . The time for speculation has passed. First, we need to know if the *Ayacucho City* carries the anthrax. Then, if she does . . .'

The Lion smiled a little, and raised its head hopefully, '. . . perhaps MOD would consider a brief. For B.M.S.N.C.?'

*

Leaning over the promenade deck rail I watched as the yellow glow of St. Vincent faded into the darkness astern. Gradually the peace of a big ship at sea closed around me with only the soft rush of the waves along the huge steel hull and, from the boat deck above, the

95

muffled purr of the diesel exhaust gases as the funnel threw them high in the black velvet sky.

She was a nice, modern ship, the *Ayacucho City*, even though she was a bastard product of no mercantile marine with her Liberian registration and her Greco-Jewish ownership. Her master was a Greek as well – Captain Constantine Argenti of the black beard, the voracious appetite and the bloody terrible English. But I liked him, and was more convinced than ever that neither he nor his slap-happy crew, mostly Greek nationals also, had enough fanatical hatred of anything, never mind their own Israeli oppos, to hit them with the horrors of Anthrax-B.

I had one small reservation. An irritating little memory which kept niggling at the back of my mind. A remark J.C. had passed. About being wary of the Greeks who come bearing gifts. . . .

If that meant anything I could be in dead trouble should they find out why I was aboard. In fact – I could be dead!

Two hundred feet ahead of me the foc'slehead look-out struck eight bells while, over my head, the mutter of alien voices drifted down from the bridge. Third Officer Mikkos was taking over the eight to twelve watch from my contemporary, First Mate Grigorios Kanellopoulos . . . Oh Jesus but we had it good in the British Merchant Navy which was full of blokes called Smith and Brown, and Alf and Bert.

I grinned bitterly towards the coast of Portugal and, turning away from the rail, made my way forward along the dimly-lit alleyway towards the saloon and dinner.

*

Aboard the *Ayacucho City* there was never any question of the propriety of waiting for the master to take his place before dinner was served – old Argenti was always there first anyway, with knife and fork cocked for action.

The smell of garlic as I entered made its usual assault on my palate and I just smiled weakly when the Old Man waved happily and bellowed, 'Siddown, siddown Mistra Cabel. Is *dolmathes* for the special chow tonight. Bluddy good, yes?'

The sloe-eyed fourth mate, who reminded me of the kind of kid you expect to see wearing a goatskin in the middle of a flock of Greek sheep, stared dispassionately at me over what looked ridiculously like a plateful of stewed vine leaves, and carried on chewing stolidly.

I queried, '*Dolmathes*, Captain?'

The black beard waggled with the enthusiasm of the true gastronome. 'You will bluddy love it up, Mistra Cabel. Is the specialisation of my galley man. Is the stuffed vine leafs, you know?'

But then again, I should have guessed!

Staring at the glass of wine the steward poured I thought how much it looked like blood and half wished, right then, that it was – preferably J.C.'s. Or McReadie's would have been an admirable substitute. I shouldn't have been here at all, I was an ignorant

D

bloody sailorman, not a suavely smooth espionage type. They needed Super Spy for this job, with a bagful of cigarette lighter machine guns and thermo-nuclear pencils and escape helicopters you ran up out of an imitation umbrella. And the impossible luck that only a novelist's pen can arrange.

But J.C. had said it was a ship that was suspect, and only a seaman could investigate a ship. I'd thought happily about how indispensable I was aboard *Commander* and mentally wished Commander McReadie, R.N. *bon voyage* to Halifax – then J.C. had smiled his skeletal, humourless smile and added, 'McReadie needs some sea time and can easily cope as *Commander*'s mate until you rejoin her in Haifa, Cable. Now, when you get aboard the Liberian . . .'

Then the proposal he outlined regarding my potential skullduggery aboard Captain Constantine Argenti's cosmopolitan command started the fingers of fear digging deeper in my belly than ever before, while the instructions about the action I was to take if I confirmed the presence of Anthrax-B seemed to make even that Kamikaze co-pilot a better risk for a life insurance policy . . .

. . . and the blood turned abruptly back into wine as the *Ayacucho City*'s only other passenger sat down beside me and said, 'Not eating, Mister Cable? Actually the ship rolling like this worries me a little, too.'

I snapped out of my nightmare reverie, but I didn't stop feeling scared as hell.

Because the other passenger had the beautiful,

haunting witchery of a Siren, those sea-nymphs of mythology whose singing lured unwary sailors to their death. Her father was a specialist in one of the Edinburgh hospitals, but she still retained her Jordanian passport. In fact, she'd used it recently when a ship called the *Attawapiskat River* landed her in the Port of Quebec not so very long ago.

Her name was Fathi al-Rana'i.

And she had bloody lovely legs!

*

The canvas hatch cover was as stiff and unyielding as a skin of concrete and I felt a fingernail split agonisingly while I struggled to turn one corner back.

Under my feet the steel deck rose and fell steadily as the *Ayacucho City* butted her flared bows into the rising westerly swell sweeping through the Straits. Occasionally, like an eerie grey phantom in the blackness, the seventh wave of a seventh wave reared ominously above bulwark level then fell away with a frustrated hiss into the tumbled white maelstrom of our wake.

The foc'slehead bell rang distantly. Two strikes, then two, and two. Six bells – Eleven p.m. I didn't have much time before the watch changed.

I was right aft, wrestling by touch with all the nervous disabilities of a blind robber, trying urgently to break open as much of number six hatch cover as was required to gain access to the grain below. I had to touch that, too – gather it into the plastic container the bacteriological warfare people had supplied.

99

The old familiar fingers of revulsion started clawing at my gut until I had to stop for a moment to draw a deep breath of courage. Oh, they'd assured me – in an irresponsibly casual way to my hypersensitive mind – that I was 'Safe as making sandcastles on the beach, old boy. Just don't be tempted to have a nibble, eh?'

But I still couldn't shake the image from my brain of a photograph showing a diseased, suppurating thing in what was once the shape of a man. And I knew that, after I'd finished, I would sit through the rest of the night just staring and staring into the mirror, wondering and waiting for the first hideous sores to appear on the much loved image of Brevet Cable, bloody Hero.

Which, on reflection, was an epitaph worthy of the ironic McReadie himself, seeing the only reason I was here was that I didn't have the guts to refuse.

A second fingernail splintered and I started to curse savagely under my breath as I realised even more water-swollen wedges would have to come out before I could free the hellish flax cover which seemed to have developed a single-mindedness of its own.

'Fuggin' Greek . . . fuggin' useless . . . fuggin' . . . sailors!' I whispered hysterically as I kicked at the stolid wedges while all the time throwing wild, nervous glances forward towards the dark bulk of the centre-castle accommodation as it threw an uneasily rolling silhouette of boats and ventilators and davits and swinging masts against the tumbled Mediterranean sky.

Abruptly the steel hatch bar jumped out of its

keepers of its own accord and the whole twelve foot length clattered to the deck with a clang that echoed like a propeller dropping off in dry dock. I froze with the spontaneous rigidity of a natural coward and awaited the onslaught of the maritime Greek hordes.

But nothing happened.

Eventually I risked a slight movement – I breathed – and thought with a mixture of relief and professional critique that the somnolent Third Mate Mikkos was one officer of the watch I'd rather see unemployed than steaming towards me at seventeen knots in charge of a big ship.

I ever so carefully lifted the starboard side hatch bar to the deck and, rolling the now docile canvas further back, uncovered the heavy slab of timber still remaining between me and the cargo.

Fumbling blindly I found the recessed ring, then slipping a rope's end through, braced my legs and strained until the blood pounded in my ears. Suddenly the timber lifted and came with a rush, riding up towards me like a gigantic surf board. Sitting down abruptly with agonisingly scraped shins I swore with all the finesse gained through twenty years of sea time at J.C. and McReadie and the Egyptians, and at the silly, ignorant bastard who'd designed these ships in the first place.

Then I cautiously leaned over the steel coaming and looked down. Number six was topped right up and, only about four feet below me and billowing away into the stale mustiness of the hold, I could dimly see the

surface of the grain. It seemed incredible, utterly in-
conceivable, that within this innocuous cereal lurked
the possible destruction of a whole nation.

Hitler would have approvingly called it 'The Final
Solution'.

A microscopic, stick-shaped bacilli that could eter-
nally quench the light from the Star of David.

It could quench Brevet Cable's feeble glimmer too.
And I was only C. of E.

I leaned forward with the gagging constriction rising
in my throat. A runnel of sweat ran down my nose and
plopped into the hold. When it touched my hand the
grain felt dry as the dust of a centuries old corpse. . . .

Oh, *Jesus*!

A torchlight flashed briefly from the high centrecastle.

Then someone started to descend the well deck
ladder towards me.

*

There's an old sailorman's adage — 'When in danger or
in doubt, starb'd your helm and go about'. But it
didn't apply to my particular hand in the jam situation.
I couldn't run aft because that meant climbing the poop
ladder under the bright glow of the adjacent bulkhead
light. I daren't risk ploughing noisily through the
unseen mess of winches and wire ropes over to the port
side. And I certainly couldn't move forward towards
the approaching flashlight.

And anyway, the hatch was so wide open that if he didn't actually see it he'd bloody well fall down it. I only had one alternative.

Live now . . . die later.

I dived headfirst into the shifting mattress of the grain, scrabbled wildly to pull the canvas cover over the gap, and lay curled in a shuddering, foetal ball of jangling nerve ends while, all over my prickling skin, a hundred million anthrax bacilli seemed to crawl and slime and creep.

And, over my head, the shuffle of feet abruptly stopped.

Which, of course, they always do. In films. Except this wasn't a film, it was happening to me, Brevet Cable, and I suddenly wanted to scream for that was the moment that I knew the cargo of the *Ayacucho City* really *was* going to kill me. And in a lot less than twelve hours.

When I found myself drowning in five fathoms of grain!

Trapped in the claustrophobic blackness of the hold I could feel the millions of granules around me moving, constantly shifting and tumbling and sucking. A dehydrated quicksand with an almost supernatural energy of its own as it vibrated unceasingly. . . .

. . . Vibration? Oh Christ! I suddenly understood why the surface under me was so unstable. Because there *was* a form of life beneath me as I heard the sound so familiar that I was normally unaware of it – in the constant rumble of the *Ayacucho City*'s twin phosphor-bronze propellers as they churned through the cold sea below.

And as they also churned the column of grain filling number six hold into a constantly searching, simmering, insubstantial coffin.

Dully I was conscious of the scrape of a match above me, then the footsteps moved metallically aft, towards the poop. Of course – it was only the stand-by duty quartermaster taking the taffrail log reading. I started to flounder and sob as I felt the hellish granules working down my neck and into my hair. My fingers clawed vainly at the smooth steel walls of the inboard coaming but, inexorably, the voracious mass was closing over my head.

I sensed, rather than heard, the returning footsteps . . . and I was going to die anyway. I opened my mouth to shout, to beg, for release – even if it would only be through a shot in the forehead to prove McReadie had been right – but the anonymous crewman just kept on going right past the place where I was dying . . .

. . . while I found I couldn't cry out after all.

Because the smothering, encroaching carpet filled my nose and eyes, and ears. And my silently screaming mouth.

And Anthrax-B was incurable after entry into the digestive tract.

*

I remember flailing my arms in an agony of hysteria even though my mind kept shrieking 'If the cargo's already contaminated just sink, Cable, you poor doomed bastard. Just sink and choke until your lungs burst, 'cause it'll be the easiest death you've got left . . .!'

But I also remember the wonderful pain of a split knuckle as my hand suddenly slammed against something sharp and cold and hard, and I felt my fingers finally clutch at the steel rungs of the vertical ladder.

I remember dragging myself inch by tortured inch until I could turn back the canvas shroud above me and draw great, sobbing gouts of wonderfully cool air. Then I half ran, half stumbled towards the dim line of the bulwarks and, hanging unheedingly out over the rushing, tumbling crash of the sea, I forced my fingers down my throat, vomiting dreadfully while the red haze shuttered down over my screwed-up eyes and the tears of utter misery and fright ran down my dusty face.

But I didn't really need any help to be violently sick.

Not while my image-obsessed imagination could already feel the great spreading sores and the obscene degeneration of the flesh that marked me as a dying man.

*

By five in the morning I was back in my cabin with another two random samples from numbers one and four holds – and a nervous twitch that would have won the sympathy of a Gestapo interrogator. In fact, anyone but J.C.

I staggered into the shower room, still shaken by an

occasional tremor of involuntary revulsion, and stripped off every stitch of clothing then, bundling it all together, un-dogged the port and shoved the whole bloody lot through into the sea.

It didn't make me feel one bit better though, even after I'd soaped and scrubbed myself practically raw. I knew that, if the *Ayacucho City*'s cargo was to be contaminated – which meant that, unless they'd failed during the loading phase, it must be already because there was no other opportunity now without the assistance of the Liberian's crew – then the bacilli was deep into my system, and I was beyond help.

But I still scrubbed and scrubbed like a demented dhobi-wallah.

Finally I dragged myself back to my cabin and slipped into the soothing coolness of my pyjamas. Why, I don't really know, I certainly wasn't going to be sleeping – unless it was permanently.

Then I lifted my suitcase on to the bed. There was still one more duty to perform before I could settle down to the mirror death-watch on Brevet Cable.

There were two small yellow canisters hidden under the dirty shirts in my case. I removed one and, opening it, slipped the three sample containers into the lined interior. I triggered a recessed micro-switch and watched momentarily as a tiny green neon winked at me, then, ever so carefully, closed it again.

I glanced at my watch – 5.48 a.m. Easing my door open I moved quietly out into the stateroom corridor.

Everything was quiet and still apart from the anonymous creaks from the now sluggishly rolling ship. I stepped out on to the after end of the promenade deck and saw, close on our port beam, the hugely comforting bulk of Gibraltar Rock with its necklace of lights strung round the base and, high above me, the ruby red crown of aerial warning beacons.

I wondered if I'd ever see it again.

Then, raising the precious canister on which so much depended, I performed the only really flawless part of my mission.

I threw it into the bloody sea.

*

My appearance at the breakfast table was purely for the sake of appearances, hunger had nothing to do with it whatsoever. I didn't need any convincing to know that the condemned man didn't eat a hearty breakfast after all – even without having to contend with the homicidally perverted ingenuity of the *Ayacucho City*'s galley.

The happy captain was there before the cook as usual. When I poked my head round the door his bass roar cut through the babble of Greek small talk from the junior engineers' table. 'Good morning, Mistra Cabel my friend. Come, siddown for breaking your fast, ha!'

Sliding cautiously into my place I cast an apprehensive eye towards the serving hatch. Old Constantine performed his inevitable early warning on the menu. 'My galley man, he done himself up a treat for chow...'

I blinked disbelievingly at the plate the steward slipped before me while the Old Man watched with proprietary pride. '. . . is a real bluddy surprise, no?'

And I couldn't have suggested a more appropriate adjective. I don't like curry, not even for dinner!

*

I wasn't feeling one bit happier when, by midday, my constant scrutiny in the mirror hadn't revealed the slightest traces of incipient anthrax. By then I'd completely convinced myself that the Professor had specified twelve *days*, not hours. I was, therefore, quietly composing myself for a dignified passing-over when I hauled myself up the after ladder to the boat deck and stared dispiritedly along our ruler-straight wake towards where, six hours and one hundred miles ago, I'd ditched the little yellow canister.

If the Navy had done their job properly I didn't have very long to wait before I knew whether I had any future left to plan for. I hoped to God the Grey Funnel Line were a bloody sight more efficient than I was.

It took another forty-five minutes of black despair before the door to the W.T. room opened and the little Greek radio operator wandered out in red striped pyjamas and a uniform cap. I wasn't offended at all though – I was only interested in the buff envelope he held in his hand. It either contained my pardon or my death warrant. And who cares what the executioner wears when it's eight o'clock in the morning?

He saw me staring at him and grinned sheepishly. 'I am off watch but still I hear the calling sign of the chip, Mister Cabble. . . .'

Chip . . . ? Ship . . . ? Oh, the hell with it! I mumbled 'For me?' and grabbed the cablegram, trying to look pleasantly surprised. Then I remembered he hadn't actually suggested it was, and just hoped he hadn't noticed the slip. He looked a bit nonplussed but eventually shrugged and shambled back off to his radio room, scratching furiously, while I tore the envelope open in clumsy haste.

The message didn't say very much. CABLE B. MV AYACUCHO CITY J5KS. TEST—NEGATIVE STOP SIGNED MAC.

It was more than enough. It told me I could think about living again!

For a few moments all I could do was hang over the rail and grin like an idiot. And think how lovely the sun was. And wish I hadn't ditched a thirty guinea suit through the bloody port hole last night when all the time I'd really known there was nothing to worry about. A catspaw of wind ruffled the glassy swell and I turned to let it play on my face.

I felt pretty good. For a few minutes.

Looking forward I could see the white cap cover of the officer of the watch as he paced idly back and forward between the wheelhouse door and the bridge wing. Suddenly, through the relief, I felt a stab of jealousy for all the familiar things I used to do before I got caught up in this hellish tidal wave of conjecture about the Glen Dhearg affair. Dammit, here I was stuck on a bloody floating dietician's nightmare in the middle of the Mediterranean, suffering from nervous exhaustion through worrying about something which probably didn't even exist aboard any ship in any ocean, other than in McReadie's conclusion-raddled mind . . .

. . . then I glanced over the rail and caught sight of a pretty, raven haired girl with gorgeous legs, and I knew I was still wrong and McReadie was right, and that – somehow – the *Ayacucho City* was being used as the carrier after all. Because coincidence just couldn't stretch far enough to explain the presence of Miss Fathi al-Rana'i, late of Edinburgh, Scotland and en route to Haifa. Via Halifax.

But as the stuff wasn't in the cargo then there were only two other possibilities – either the Jordanian girl was scheduled to contaminate the hold single handed before we raised Haifa, or I had Captain Constantine Argenti figured wrongly for the happy go lucky old gannet he appeared to be.

I stared moodily out over the twinkling blue swell and felt the ship roll gently under my feet. It still didn't make sense. According to the C.B.W. experts the only way the grain could be efficiently adulterated was by spraying the top surface of each hold with a dilution of the missing Anthrax-B. Twenty-four hours later and the insidious bacilli would have contaminated every granule where it would lie dormant for ever – or until such time as the salivated warmth of the human intestine re-activated it, and caused it to multiply, and devour the blood cells, and liquify the still living tissue. . . .

Involuntarily my already scarred hands gripped the rail too tightly, the pain from my broken nails dewing my forehead with cold sweat. But I'd suddenly realised that, even though I was temporarily as virile and healthy as ever, I was still scheduled to be a dead man before the Liberian arrived under the red haze over Israel.

Because the slim, slightly built girl below me could never have hoped to move the heavy hatch covers alone, and certainly not during the clandestinely dark hours of the night when such an operation needs the hand of a professional seaman.

Which meant that the Greeks *must* be involved, after all.

And who wants a witness to genocide?

*

It took me a long time to decide what to do, even when I knew I had no choice. I had to shout for help from J.C., and not just to save my own skin.

At least that's what I tried to convince myself while I struggled to draft some kind of signal that wouldn't excite the curiosity of young Pyjama Suit in the W.T. room but would, at the same time, cause the *Ayacucho City* to be stopped and searched from truck to keel long before she ever got into Israeli waters.

I'd stopped caring about the legal and International implications of such a piratical act. The Admiral was right, it didn't need a politician to guess that, if Captain Argenti took this ship inside Haifa breakwater – whether or not we tipped off the Israeli authorities at the last minute – then if the anthrax didn't decimate the Jewish people the fall-out from the possible following thermo-nuclear holocaust very well might. Along with a few million Englishmen, and Indonesians, and Americans and Rumanians and Russians and . . .

. . . the pencil snapped abruptly in my hands. It was all predicted already. In the Bible's Revelation.

And it was bloody ironic that the Holy Land itself was chosen for the Armageddon.

I finished writing the message and looked at it doubtfully. HAPPY BIRTHDAY TO VICTOR STOP SIGNED UNCLE BREV. Was it enough? Or would McReadie and J.C. just think I'd flipped my lid and ignore it, assuming that the *Ayacucho City* was clean and that it was only Chief Officer Cable who was living in a fantasy world now?

Mind you, they'd soon twig all wasn't right the moment they came aboard in Haifa to find I wasn't – aboard, I mean.

But that didn't give me the slightest lift of satisfaction.

*

We were entering the Sicilian Narrows as I walked up to the radio room and over to starboard I could see the thirty-one square miles of Pantellaria shimmering in the heat haze. Only about three and a half steaming days left before we raised Haifa. I knew something had to happen soon.

The little Sparks was even less the sartorial seadog as I entered to find him with feet propped up on the transmitting table and a lurid Greek Beano in his hands . . . he didn't even have his cap on this time. When he saw me he clutched the comic warily, almost as if he expected me to grab it like I'd snatched McReadie's cable, but I just smiled reassuringly and proffered the signal form.

I left him tapping with deft professionalism, lips carefully forming the unaccustomed English letter sequences, and stepped back out on to the boat deck feeling a slight sense of relief in that at least I'd taken some positive action to keep me alive.

Yet would they understand the meaning hidden under the nonsensical text? HAPPY BIRTHDAY TO VICTOR . . . when there wasn't any Victor.

But Victor was the N.A.T.O. phonetic for the letter 'V'.

And 'V' in the Seamen's International Code means – I require assistance!

*

Eight hours later and it was 'eyes down for dinner' again. And the suddenly sinister Captain Argenti was still pretending to be as gastronomically solicitous as ever. He beamed at me through the blood red rivulets of his emptied wine glass.

'You enjoy your bluddy good chow, Mistra Cabel?'

I hadn't actually, partly because I hadn't even known what I'd been eating for the last fifteen minutes, but I felt this was the wrong time to make him dislike me so I nodded emphatically. He grinned delightedly and thumped the table with all the boisterousness of a baby gorilla. 'I tell you I gotta galley man is a dazzling bobby, hah? I love him up all the time.'

But I think it was his English, not his sexual appetite, which was at fault.

I took a deep breath and turned to the seat next to me. The lovely limpid black eyes of the girl Fathi looked back at me expressionlessly. Ever since I'd come aboard I'd been trying unsuccessfully to get under her skin, prise out even one small clue that might help me sort out the bloody mess I'd got myself into. And I had a cold, prickly feeling that this was to be my last chance before death-time.

She just smiled when I said, perhaps rather too pointedly, 'Forgive me, Miss al-Rana'i, but isn't it a little strange that a Jordanian should be going to Haifa? I mean, you don't ... ah ... get on terribly well, do you?'

'With the Israelis, Mister Cable ...?' She shrugged, '... I'm afraid that, since the earthquake, our relations are somewhat better than before. ...'

'*Afraid*?' I looked surprised, 'Why? Because your relationship with Israel has improved?'

She bit her lip and I couldn't help thinking how damnably attractive she was. 'Would *you* be pleased to think of all those poor people – Arabs too, Mister Cable – buried alive? Of course I'm afraid.'

Touché! I probed a bit harder. 'But Haifa? Why not straight into Aqaba? Into a Jordanian port?'

This time she smiled with genuine amusement. 'I'm tempted to suggest that you study your geography a little more, Mister Cable. Aqaba is Jordanian, yes. In fact, it's my country's only major sea port, but it is entered from the Red Sea, not the Mediterranean.'

I looked idiotically embarrassed and shook my head in pretended confusion. 'Of course. . . . And Nasser closed the Suez Canal. I forgot.'

The beautiful mask slipped fractionally. 'The *Israelis* closed the Canal, Mister Cable. Not Colonel Nasser.'

I experimentally touched the exposed nerve again. 'What's wrong, Miss al-Rana'i? Are you an anti-Zionist at heart, or is it mandatory for every Arab to blame the Jews for everything just to give the late Papa Nasser an excuse for losing the Six Day War?'

She pushed her chair back and stood up. I could see the active dislike in her eyes and, strangely, it hurt me very much. But I'd gone too far to re-establish diplomatic relations so I just grinned aggressively as she walked statuesquely to the door.

Stopping, she said slowly, 'The Jews are pillagers of my people's land. No true Arab could find room in their heart for anything but hatred of those who took Palestine away from us . . .'

She hesitated before she finally went out. '. . . but I am a Jordanian even before I am an Arab, Mister

Cable. And because of that I can find no respect for Gamal Abdel Nasser or those others of that Egyptian Council who caused the loss to my nation of the City of Jerusalem!'

And then the master of the *Ayacucho City*, who'd been very, very quiet while the girl was in the saloon, really demolished my abruptly tottering web of suspicion.

By spitting on the deck beside his chair, and saying grimly, 'Is a bluddy Arab bitch. Maybe I haf to passage them on my chip . . . but I no haf to fuggin' love them up. Not for no bluddy hand-out to the proud Israeli peoples!'

And I knew, beyond any doubt, that he meant it. Every last distorted syllable.

*

It felt wonderful to be on the bridge of a ship at sea again, even a foreigner like the *Ayacucho City*. For a few minutes I just hung over the bridge front and breathed the seventeen knot wind of our passage as it curled over the furled canvas dodger. The velvety blackness of the night seemed very protective as I watched the warm yellow glow of the masthead light spiralling gently against the canopy of winking stars.

I wondered if death could ever be as peaceful.

A movement in the darkness beside me and Captain Argenti's voice, strangely quiet, broke into my reverie. 'You like it, Mistra Cabel? Up here in the sky.'

I glanced down, over the bridge wing, to where the

whispering sea glided sixty feet below, and was oddly touched by the Captain's uncharacteristic poetry. 'I like it very much, Captain Argenti.'

I could sense him nodding slowly. 'Is good. Being a sailorman.'

And I started worrying again, and hoping J.C. would do something soon, because I just didn't know what there was about this strange ship and the in-tangibly inconsistent people who sailed in her that made me so nervous.

I just knew I still had cause to worry.

We'd come up to the bridge immediately after dinner. The Old Man had shaken off his irritation at the girl Fathi and had boomed cheerfully, 'You ever been on the bridge of a big chip, Mistra?'

I'd said 'no' because I was an earthquake expert on paper, then, to consolidate my assumed lack of maritime knowledge, had added, 'And I've always wanted to see how you anchor at night. When it gets too dark for you to see where you're going.'

He'd laughed hugely all the way up to the boat deck and told me I was, 'The most bluddy funniest of chaps.'

Just forward of our port beam I could see the eastern tip of Sicily ending in the faint loom of Cape Passero Light. I gestured vaguely towards the silhouetted peaks in the darkness. 'Is that land, Captain?'

'Is Sicilia, Mistra Cabel. Is full of the bandido. A no good bluddy place, yes?'

Above us and forward of the softly purring funnel I

could discern the monotonous sweep of the rotating radar scanner. Captain Argenti was obviously a cautious man who took full advantage of the electronic age. He must have sensed me looking up for he said, 'Is the radar. For seeing in the bad visibility I bluddy love it up. You would like to watch?'

I followed him into the wheelhouse thinking he had one hell of a varied sex life.

Inside the wheelhouse, sheltered from even the incidental reflection of the moonless sky, it was so black you could almost have touched it. Only the faint glow from the binnacle picked out the olive skinned high-lights on the lounging Greek quartermaster's face as he stood, legs easily straddled, at the wheel. Out on the starboard wing, seen faintly through the open doorway, the dim figure of Third Officer Mikkos hung boredly over the bridge front. I hoped he was a bloody sight more wide awake than he had been during my noisy spell of breaking and entering on the after deck. The Sicilian Narrows weren't the place for a watchkeeping somnambulist.

Argenti's voice cut across the faint click of the gyro compass and I turned to see the Captain's craggy face underlit by the eerie green glow from the hooded radar console. He seemed hugely Mephistophelian as he smiled to show the flash of strong teeth against the black frame of his beard.

'This is Captain Argenti's television set. Is a good picture, but the story she is bluddy slow, yes?'

He laughed enormously as I moved over and peered

down at the familiar screen. I tried to sound over-awed. 'Good God . . . and that lighter green line, is that the land then?'

'To port – your left hand side, Mistra Cabel – that is the coast of Sicilia, yes.'

The gorilla fingers clicked the ranging switch with surprising gentleness and the screen opened up to show a smaller image of Sicily but with another, less conspicuous, land mass to starboard. The Captain murmured, 'Malta. Where your British Navy once was the top chaps. We are now passing between the two places, you understand?'

I nodded and wondered hopefully if the British Navy was still around, preferably steaming towards Brevet Cable in a County Class guided missile destroyer. I noticed several blips indicating other ships in the area. I also noted, with detached interest, that one small contact was lying almost dead ahead and about three miles away, but surely even the weary Mikkos would have her under visual observation by now as her lights crossed our path.

We talked in low tones for a few more minutes while I just absorbed the peaceful atmosphere, then Argenti moved out to the starboard wing and I made to follow. For some reason I gave a last glance into the Decca console and stopped abruptly. The image was more or less as it had been last time other than that the surrounding shipping contacts had changed their dispositions to us slightly as they also moved through the water.

All except one.

The little blip that had been across our course still was. And she hadn't moved at all.

I walked quickly out to stand behind Argenti and the Third Mate, eyes searching anxiously for the running lights of the other vessel that must, by now, be distinctly seen . . . yes, there she was! Dead ahead and, maybe, one and a half miles distant.

The funny feeling came back in my belly. Was this what I'd been praying for? Had J.C. and McReadie acted on my camouflaged S.O.S.? I was sure of one thing, though – whatever was waiting for us out there was a damned sight smaller than any destroyer.

The Old Man grunted irritably. 'Is maybe one little bluddy fisher boat but for that I have to take my chip off her course. Is a bastard, eh?'

He could have been right at that. A lot of fishing craft just sit tight and let the other bloke do the driving. But they usually showed a tricoloured light when trawling or, in the case of drifters, two white lights with the lower indicating the direction of the net. And the vessel ahead was just showing the usual white masthead lamp plus a red port running light, which meant she was passing across our bows from right to left.

I noticed Mikkos glance apprehensively at the Captain but Argenti just glowered ahead and was obviously content to let the Third Mate earn his watchkeeping drachmas. Finally the kid moved into the wheelhouse and I caught a low babble of Greek. Then the *Ayacucho City*'s foremast cut a few degrees to starboard as we altered course to pass behind the target ship.

Which was a perfectly ordinary manoeuvre, carried out a thousand times at sea every night.

Until the red light ahead was joined by a green starboard one and, suddenly, we had a vessel now only a mile distant heading straight for us on a collision course!

I started feeling very glad I was only a passenger and didn't work here. No one aboard a ten thousand ton freighter relishes playing patsy with some homicidal navigator in the middle of the night. I also felt a faint surge of optimism – whoever was arsing about ahead was doing it deliberately, and there was only one reason why they should pick on the *Ayacucho City*. Mentally I started packing my gear for the transhipment I'd been looking forward to with such nervous anticipation.

I nearly grinned openly when, without warning, the red light snapped out completely and the outrageous little ship in front showed she was now steaming back across our bows on a reciprocal course which *still* kept her dead ahead even though the *Ayacucho City* was swinging harder and harder under starboard helm.

Captain Argenti bellowed the Greek equivalent to 'Jesus fuggin' Christ!' and kicked the wooden bridge front in a surfeit of Mediterranean frustration. Then he barged into the wheelhouse and, grabbing little Mikkos by the scruff of the neck, turfed him out on to the wing.

I presumed, with a certain lascivious satisfaction, that this was the Liberian Merchant Navy's way of relieving the watchkeeper. Then I started feeling a bit sorry for the unlucky Third Mate, I knew just how he felt.

The Old Man yelled at the poor bloody helmsman too, like he was a relative of the mad mariner out there; then, as the ship's head steadied on a defeated heading towards the other vessel, the Captain grabbed the brass telegraph handles and rang for 'Stop engines'.

I was trying to peer through the darkness to make out the silhouette of the intruder when, with painful suddenness, I was blinded by the beam of a powerful searchlight as it spluttered into incandescent life and trained full on our bridge.

And the high pitched shriek of a switched-on loud hailer prefaced the very English voice which queried flatly, 'What ship?'

*

I was still stumbling around trying to regain what little night vision I had left as the huge bulk of the Captain pounded past me and leant right out over the wing, trying to shield his eyes to see behind that bloody impenetrable searchlight.

And Constantine Argenti didn't need a loud hailer. 'What you bluddy mean, asking me what chip, hah? I don't need to bluddy tell nobody what chip I got. And why you make me stop my engines an' shine the bluddy big light in my faces . . .!'

The disembodied electronic voice cut harshly across the water, stemming the Old Man's flow of outraged invective. 'This is Her Majesty's patrol craft *Diomede*. Lieutenant Commander Marsham, Royal Navy . . . I intend to board you, Captain. Perhaps you would be good enough to prepare your pilot ladder immediately.'

Argenti's mouth worked soundlessly for several moments. Even to my prejudiced mind the enormity of what was happening came as quite a shock now it was actually in motion. I was witnessing the commencement of what must eventually snowball into the biggest International maritime scandal since the U.S.S. *Pueblo* affair. The legal and diplomatic implications would reverberate throughout history, made even more suspect by virtue of the British Government's having to conceal their real reasons for such an action.

Eventually the Captain found his voice again. 'You . . . you do not board this vessel. Is a Liberian chip. Is registered in the Republic of Liberia. And I, Constantine Argenti, I am a Greek natural . . . isa non of the Royal Navy's bluddy business, hah?'

The two vessels were nearly stopped now, with only the slightest movement of water along our white boot topping. It was deathly quiet and dark as the crypt outside the periphery of the searchlight's glare, apart from the occasional blink of Cape Passero now well astern on the invisible horizon.

Diomede's hailer snapped on again. 'I am well aware of your Flag, Captain, and your protest has been duly noted. I am, however, acting in the name of Her Britannic Majesty's Government. . . . You will please prepare to receive my boarding party at once. I say again . . . at *once*, Captain!'

It struck me then that Lieutenant Commander Marsham, Royal Navy, had picked the right vocation but the wrong employer. Unless they'd designed a swastika into the White Ensign since I'd last seen it. But who was I to look a gift horse in the mouth? That was Brevet Cable's salvation out there, and it also struck me that old Argenti was perhaps acting out of rather more than outraged indignation – like a man with something to hide? Ship's masters are intensely jealous of the protection given to them by their Flags but he must have known he would finally win, assuming he was in the right.

If he was? It was a purely academic consideration, now that the moment of truth had arrived.

He pounded the teak rail angrily. 'I do nothing until I have taken my owner's instructions. I do not let you come aboard my chip. These is International waters, Commander, and for you to threaten me is act of piracy, hah? Piracy, you understand? Is bluddy not under the Law. . . . We go now, an' Captain Constantine Argenti say *that* to the Royal British bluddy Navy. Hah!'

And *that* could have been interpreted as an International sign in any language!

Argenti spat hawkingly over the wing and turned his back on the Royal Navy. I felt a chill of concern when

124

he spoke abruptly, in English, 'Full speed ahead on the both engines!'

The white-faced Mikkos hesitated fractionally and I saw his big brown cow's eyes reflecting the glare from outboard, then he shrugged imperceptibly and swung the engine room telegraphs sharply back, then forward. Almost immediately the answering clang came from below and the *Ayacucho City* started to throb urgently under the slowly gathering revolutions below her counter.

I began to feel scared again. Just how far was the Navy authorised to go? Stopping a merchantman on the High Seas is bad enough, but if she refuses to stop. . . . I started to edge towards the extreme wing of the bridge. Maybe I should jump for it? Get out while I still had the chance of being pulled out of the water? Then I glanced down and saw the black, black sea churning sixty feet below, and I knew I didn't have the guts to go over. . . .

But I suddenly found out that the Royal Navy were prepared to go just as far as they had to anyway, and without the preliminary conventions . . .

. . . when the vicious slam of a shot from H.M.S. *Diomede* merged into the super-heated flash of a direct hit on the *Ayacucho City*'s foc'slehead!

*

I remember hearing the smash of glass as shrapnel atomised one of the wheelhouse windows, then I was hugging the wooden decking in shocked reaction while

Third Mate Mikkos proved by one milli-second he was a bigger coward than me.

Until someone started screaming horribly from the fore part of the ship, and I forgot all about the Navy as I stared into the Greek kid's terrified eyes and shouted, 'Jesus, but there was a man on the foc'slehead! You had a bloody look-out stationed forr'ad, didn't you ... ?'

But old Argenti just roared like a wounded bull, slammed the telegraphs to 'Stop engines' and bellowed 'Mayday! I want the Mayday S.O.S. to be transmitted ... I want on International frequency the message, "My chip attacked Royal Navy vesse ... No! Is *by* Royal Navy vessel? Position ... position twelve mile east sou' east Cape Passero! Sent on open R.T.... !'

The flat English voice cut across to us again. 'I have instructions either to board or sink you, Captain. I must also advise you not to attempt to use your radio at this time. ... Do *not* transmit by radio. And now, the pilot ladder, please. Over your starboard side forward.'

The hailer snapped off as the wounded man started screaming again from the foc'slehead. Argenti turned slowly and I saw his shoulders sag. When he saw me watching he didn't seem angry any more, just defeated. If I hadn't been so damnably relieved I would have been sorry to see the old Greek's ebullience so brutally dampened.

'I have the feeling, Mistra Cabel,' he said in a low voice, 'that maybe it is for you my poor sailorman has been hurt, hah? You make me very sad to think I loved you up. As a friend.'

I just stared at him as he turned his back bitterly and reverted to Greek. Even when he had finished giving the little Mikkos instructions and the Third Mate had gone clattering nervously down the ladder I still stood there on the *Ayacucho City*'s bridge and felt the soft Mediterranean night close around me again, and watched numbly as the white finger from H.M.S. *Diomede* threw our upperworks into stark relief.

And felt very, very sad indeed.

*

By the time the Third Mate had rigged the boarding ladder over the bulwarks below me, other crewmen had carried the bloody mess that had been the foc'slehead look-out aft towards the empty cabin which served as a ship's hospital. I gazed down, still loath to leave the comforting environment of the bridge, and bit my lip as one of the Greeks hesitated, then gestured to the wounded man and shrugged hopelessly.

I wanted to shout 'Sorry, it's all been a silly mistake so put Humpty back together again . . .,' but there was still the Jordanian girl, and *someone* must have intended to help her with the anthrax I knew was aboard. But who?

The first of the R.N. boarding party swung his legs over the bulwarks and dropped lightly to the deck surrounded by a semi-circle of ominously quiet Greek sailors.

I saw the flash of gold from his uniform epaulettes and realised that Lieutenant Commander Marsham was visiting personally. A rating, cap tilted cockily forward over his eyes, followed. Then another and another until the whole party of twelve men stood warily with their backs to the still penetrating *Diomede*'s searchlight. I noticed they were all armed with sub-machine guns with the exception of the Commander, who carried a .38 Webley and Scott lanyarded round his bronzed neck.

A leading hand moved forward and, gripping the nearest Greek by the arm, roughly about turned him and pushed until the man was face down over the bulwarks with all his weight on his hands and feet splayed out behind – the classic posture for immobilising suspects. A mutter of angry protests from the other crewmen subsided into a foot-shuffling silence as the submachine gun barrels of the bluejackets jerked warningly . . . Christ, but J.C. must have laid it on thick with the Ministry of Defence to get this tough.

Two more minutes and every Greek on the Liberian's well deck was lined along the rail with other crewmen, including the engineers, being shepherded from all parts of the ship. I had to admire the Lieutenant Commander's cold efficiency. It was the first time I'd seen the Royal Navy in this kind of operation and it made me feel a lot safer just watching.

The Commander gestured and, followed by two ratings, moved aft under the break of the centrecastle, quickly making their way up to the bridge. I hoped old Argenti wouldn't do anything silly when they arrived but he was talking in low tones to the now unemployed helmsman in the wheelhouse so I couldn't make out his reactions to the scene on the foredeck.

And I didn't think this was quite the time for a Judas like me to emphasise my presence so I just stepped discreetly back into the shadows beside the chartroom door and waited impatiently for the Navy.

Suddenly the quartermaster moved out of the wheelhouse and was sliding down the ladder past me before I realised what was happening. I watched curiously as he ran aft and wondered what the urgency was. Then I heard the footsteps as the boarding party climbed the far side, port, bridge ladder. I didn't want to appear too anxious – the debonairly casual approach struck me as more in keeping with an unruffled B.M.S.N.C. cloak and dagger pundit – so I just stayed where I was to let the initial slanging match with Argenti die down.

It struck me as being rather more safely discreet, too.

The Commander had his gun out of its webbing holster as he stepped up on to the wing. I moved forward slightly to see better and watched as my huge Greek friend went angrily to meet his mentors. The familiar booming voice was back in form.

'I want you to know that I make the strongest representative to the Liberian Government, hah? And to my own Government of Hellas, also. And to the

United Nations, they will be listening to me as well also! I tell you this make the Royal British Navy into the bluddy pirates, yes? And Constantine Argenti does not love up the bluddy pirates, I warn you. . . .'

The two able seamen watched with typical British lower deck impassiveness while Commander Marsham stepped forward and saluted smartly. His tone was very correct as he spoke. 'Please accept the British Government's expression of concern at any inconvenience I may have been forced to cause you, Captain. . . .'

Argenti waved his hands excitedly. 'Inconvenie . . . I You shoot at my chip an' maybe kill one of my poor bluddy sailormans. And then you make the guns point at me on my own bridge, hah? And now are you saying you are so sorry for this. . . .'

The Commander's voice was still correct but it had an indefinable edge to it this time. 'I have reason to believe you have a passenger aboard this ship, Captain Argenti . . . A Jordanian national, probably known to you as Miss Fathi al-Rana'i.'

I admit I felt a bit hurt. They could have shown a little more concern for the well-being of Brevet Cable first. But what the hell, I was too damned glad to see J.C.'s maritime fifth cavalry to take offence. I started to make my entrance for the grand re-union scene when Argenti nodded aggressively, 'I have, yes. But does this mean that the British Navy is making war on the Jordanian peoples too, hah . . . ?'

I suddenly stopped moving and froze. Something seemed a little . . . wrong.

Because Lieutenant Commander Marsham R.N. relaxed slightly and murmured, 'I *am* glad, Captain. For a moment I was terribly afraid we might have stopped the wrong ship. . . .'

Then he deliberately shot the master of the *Ayacucho City*. Right in the pit of the stomach.

Chapter Four

During those initial moments of shock I just stayed where I was, paralysed with horror and disbelief. Yet, even then, I found myself staring at the Commander while my mind struggled to pin-point the one small physical anomaly that was worrying me so much.

While Captain Argenti shook his huge, bearded head slowly in utter incredulity, and said, 'Is Argenti's chip. Is not allowed to shoot . . . Not *Argenti*. Not on his own bridge. . . .'

But, just to show he didn't care, the Commander fired again. Twice.

It was all so bloody ridiculous, really. Like people shooting at people. In Scotland.

And Constantine Argenti still couldn't believe what was happening to him, either. Perhaps that's why he didn't just lie down and die like any other man would have done with three .38 short rounds impacted in his lower abdomen.

Instead, he only slid down against the wheelhouse door for a few seconds until the great hands clawed him back to the vertical, then – bellowing in agony-laden outrage at the men who had presumed to offend his position as master by actually shooting him aboard his own beloved chip – the gargantuan Greek stumbled towards them in an awful majesty of defiance.

Deliberately, the Commander stepped to one side as the leading hand behind him raised the barrel of his submachine gun. The single burst of fire shattered the wheelhouse side windows on either hand of Argenti while the master of the *Ayacucho City* was propelled backwards, past the steering telemotor and bright brass telegraphs and, still roaring bloody hate, backwards across the starboard wing until the outboard rail acted as a fulcrum in the small of his back and his feet came up as he tipped over, out, and down into the black sea below.

And I pressed even further into the concealing shadows, because I'd suddenly realised what it was about the captain of Her Majesty's Ship *Diomede* that had seemed so curiously out of place.

It was only a trivial little detail, really. A silly thing to notice at all, now that the killing had started.

But Lieutenant Commander Marsham, Royal Navy, wore the faintest suspicion of a hairline moustache!

*

The second rating started running through the wheelhouse towards where Argenti had disappeared over the wall. I had about two seconds left before he saw me.

And, suddenly, I didn't want to meet the Navy. Not Marsham's navy, anyway.

Because while, to neutralise the threat of Anthrax-B, it was conceivable that Their Lords of the Admiralty might have been prepared to turn a Nelsonian blind eye to H.M. Ships shooting up the odd foreign cargo boat, I knew that they would never, ever, countenance such depravity as a Royal Naval officer with a cultivated upper lip.

Not without a beard to match. Of the officially approved, M.O.D. sea-dog pattern.

So I flung myself clear over the after end of the late Captain Argenti's bridge to land with a bone jarring crash on the boat deck some ten feet below.

For some reason I didn't feel scared any more – just bloody sore. I also thought I knew why the quarter-master had done a quick flit from the wheelhouse a few minutes earlier – it must have been to carry Argenti's S.O.S. for transmission by Pyjama Suit in the W.T. cabin, and to hell with the Royal bluddy Navy.

And now I had a few things to add to the signal myself.

I clambered painfully to my feet and half ran, half limped aft to where the open port of the radio room speared a beam of yellow light across the deserted boat deck. Behind me the searchlight from the fake H.M.S. *Diomede* snapped off to be replaced by the warmer glow of the *Ayacucho City*'s own forward well deck cargo lamps.

I muttered 'Jesus!' under my breath and prayed they wouldn't switch the boat deck floods on too, exposing me like a hare over open ground.

But why light up the foredeck of the Liberian? We

must stand out like a floating Christmas tree in the night? So why take the chance of being seen . . . ?

I stopped dead as the truth struck me. Oh, my dear God – the crew. The *Ayacucho City*'s crew. They were all out there, down on the well deck, all except those who'd had the sense to hide until they knew what it was all about. And the cargo lamps would illuminate that row of splayed out men like the targets in the small arms range in B.M.S.N.C.'s Leadenhall Street basement. Like a bloody shooting gallery. . . .

Swinging round I started running hard for the W.T. room door.

I didn't stop again until I heard the two shots slamming through the dark silence. And they came from in front of me.

From inside the radio room itself.

I skidded to a halt less than three feet from the closed door. What the . . . ? Just above my head the pencil of light from the open port still beamed out to sea. Ever so cautiously I peered in in muscle-taut anticipation.

And found out just why Miss Fathi al-Rana'i had taken passage aboard the *Ayacucho City*.

*

The Greek quartermaster huddled face down on the compo deck in an untidy spread of blue-jeaned limbs. He looked even more lethargic now than he did up in the wheelhouse, but that wasn't particularly surprising. The torn black exit hole just under his left shoulder blade immediately indicated to my highly trained mind that he'd been shot. Dead.

The little wireless operator wasn't exactly a bundle of throbbing energy either, the way he was sitting all humped over in his swivel chair with his head resting tiredly on a crooked forearm. I noticed he'd at least changed his pyjamas for a very suave, silky red set which was quite appropriate, really, seeing they matched the slowly spreading pool of blood forming round the transmitting key.

I also noticed he didn't have any back to his skull, which accounted for the blood. And the lethargy.

The Jordanian girl wasn't dead, though. She was just standing there with the gun in her hand and a look of terrible revulsion in her eyes. She looked so damnably beautiful even then, and almost pitiful with the black, black hair cascading round her face, giving the impression of a pretty school-girl who'd strayed into the labyrinths of unspeakable perversions and didn't know how to get out again.

I wasn't in much of a mood to look for the extenuating circumstances though. Right then it didn't matter a damn to me whether she was a patriot, an Islamic extremist, or just a kinky dolly girl who'd killed two men for kicks.

All I knew was that I was stuck with a shipload of homicidal maniacs who went about shooting people like me with great skill and deliberacy.

And who were undoubtedly in the process of delivering Anthrax-B to the Israeli palate with the same cold, ruthless efficiency!

I risked another surreptitious glance through the port, but she was still standing with that dazed look on her face. What the hell, Miss bloody al-Rana'i couldn't feel half as shattered as little Pyjama Suit there, and the Greek with the see-through torso. I still felt cold and dead inside, not scared at all, so I wasn't really being very heroic when I started weighing up my chances of getting past the girl to the transmitter.

Then I decided I wasn't being very practical either, because she still held the gun like a professional and I didn't have the heart to make those big black eyes look any sadder when she was pointing it at me and pulling the trigger. It also crossed my mind while I was looking at the gun that, whoever was behind this operation – whether it was Sadat or Hussein, or even the whole Arab League – they'd certainly supplied the tools to do the job. Russian ammo for the Glen Dhearg attack, something a little larger and more sophisticated for stopping the *Ayacucho City*, and now the girl Fathi holding a Czechoslovakian Army Model 52 semi-automatic pistol to match the 7.63 millimetre hole in Pyjama Suit's forehead.

So exactly who *were* the faceless promoters of this crazy, genocidal venture? One thing was for sure, they must have been running on a lot of hate. . . .

Then the problem started to become more and more abstract when I heard boots clattering down the bridge ladder and running along the boat deck towards me.

A Plague of Sailors

Jesus! I'd been standing here playing Peeping Tom too long. In reality it couldn't have been more than four or five minutes since Captain Argenti had been so abruptly relieved of his command, but I should have realised they wouldn't leave the ship lying dead in the water for any longer than they had to. I remembered how I'd noticed the counterfeit H.M.S. *Diomede* on the Decca console, and how she'd stood out like a sore thumb amongst all the other traffic navigating the Sicilian Narrows simply because she was stopped.

Which meant, presumably, that they would be disposing of the embarrassment of the *Ayacucho City*'s original crew any minute now.

And me! Unless I could disappear into thin air . . . or climb that bloody wonderful vertical ladder my shoulder was nudging against, fixed to the bulkhead beside the radio room door?

But, first, I had to perform another kind of disappearing act – an illusory one. The girl undoubtedly knew I was aboard and when they finally started counting heads – or bodies? – she'd certainly query the lack of the late Brevet Cable's cadaver. So I had to supply one.

Or a substitute splash which could later be assumed to have been an unbalanced and panic stricken earthquake expert going over the wall for the deep six rather than face the alternative of a white hot shell through his tie pin.

Urgently I squeezed between the bow and stern of numbers one and three lifeboats and, grabbing for a

138

lifebuoy, smashed the bulb of the attached light float. Then I heaved it as far as I could into the concealing blackness.

I didn't even wait for the splash as I scuttled inboard again and went up the ladder fast. I was only conscious of the approaching footsteps faltering, then moving cautiously inquisitive, towards the edge of the deck I'd just left. Then I was hauling myself over the top of the ladder and thinking how grateful I was to the man who'd invented them.

Peering round I found myself lying on the rusty steel decking, sandwiched between a huge water tank aft and the raised coaming of the engine room skylight. Towering above me the great funnel moved gently against the stars, silent and dead ... like Captain Argenti of the happy, booming voice and the gargantuan appetite. Nervously I wriggled away from the engine room's glow and blinked thoughtfully. Maybe old Constantine would bluddy love me up again now? Now he knew I wasn't one of the bastards who'd killed him.

Chewing pensively at my broken nails I tried desperately to think how I was going to attempt what was obviously the most essential first move on my part – to get a Mayday transmission out from the late operator's tomb below me. Somehow I just had to let J.C. and McReadie know ... Oh, the hell with B.M.S.N.C.! Somehow I had to let *anybody* know the bloody mess I'd got myself into. Right now I'd be

happy to accept rescue from the Soviet Med Fleet
itself . . .

. . . until I heard something which made me decide
to scrap that part of my strategy too, when I caught the
splintering of glass dials and valves as the man from the
bridge eviscerated the *Ayacucho City*'s only radio
transmitter.

And muffled shouts from the forr'ad well deck
indicated that the Liberian's crew were about to be paid
off. In mid-voyage.

*

I had to do something quickly. So I did. I was sick.

It was all happening too quickly for my battered
mind. Every time I made a move I found I was one
step behind. Now there wasn't a snowball's chance in
hell of my getting an S.O.S. out, and it looked as
though my brilliantly conceived Victor signal was lying
unhelpfully in J.C.'s waste paper basket at B.M.S.N.C.

I also knew with an awful clutch of despair what was
going to happen at any moment down on the foredeck.
The submachine gunners in the jolly Jack Tar uni-
forms still stayed vividly in my memory as they stood
silently waiting in front of the line of splayed-out Greek
sailors.

And the brutality of Argenti's death. The way he
had still been roaring defiance while the heavy bullets
drove him inexorably backwards . . . and the little
Sparks who'd lost his head because of a beautiful
woman . . . literally . . .

. . . so, I was sick.

And when I'd finished retching I raised my head and saw a faint line of light along the eastern horizon. The dawn. Oh Christ, I had to move quickly, before they started the inevitable thorough search of the ship. And up here I would be as obvious as the funnel itself under the searching light of day. As obvious as the funnel itse . . . !

The funnel. The bloody lovely funnel!

I rolled over on my back and stared upwards again. Could I? Could I get up there, on top of the funnel? And, even if I did, was there enough of a lip around its periphery to conceal me? The *Ayacucho City* was a motor ship, which meant that the funnel proper was really only a comparatively narrow diameter exhaust pipe. The rest of it – the painted shell – was largely a traditional retention by the ship designers. And there was plenty of area up there for a man to lie in hiding for as long as he wanted.

But it was twenty feet of vertical steel plating. And the soft gleam of the Mediterranean dawn was already beginning to stroke the black shadows with a lighter grey tinge. I hurriedly crawled through a maze of ventilators and stanchions until eventually I was lying at the base of the huge cylinder.

And there wasn't a rung to be seen anywhere. My ladder-luck had run out.

I was beaten. And I was starting to get frightened again. I let my head sag tiredly against the rusted steel flange which formed the funnel base and listened carefully. The strain of anticipating the frightful sound of gunfire from the foredeck was beginning to leave me mentally and physically exhausted. Yet there was nothing I could do, not one solitary bloody thing, to help those poor sheep-like sailormen in front of the guns down there. All I could do was join them. When it got light. In a few more minutes. . . .

Something tickled the back of my neck. I brushed it away irritably and carried on feeling sorry for the Greeks, and the Jews, and Brevet Cable, late chief officer and earthquake expert. *Especially* Brevet Cab . . .

I rolled over and looked up, frantically trying to pierce the gloom above me. Something had touched my neck again, something soft and evasive, something which swayed with the dead roll of the ship . . . like a rope? I flapped my hands with an urgent horizontal motion, trying to catch whatever it was that had stroked me with invisible fingers.

My right hand touched, then slipped, then touched again, and I felt the length of halyard slap into my palm. I scrambled to my knees and tugged. It felt firm enough and, suddenly, I knew what it was. It must be a single whip rove through a block on top of the funnel, probably used to hoist the gear for a bosun's chair when painting time came round. Not that it did very often aboard the *Ayacucho City*. But I should worry – if I could climb it.

And if it was strong enough to prevent me from crashing backwards into twenty feet of space, then through the glass skylight and maybe another sixty feet down past those tiers of shiny silver engine room ladders to the steel bedplates of the ship.

And also *if* the gunmen on the bridge less than a spit away didn't notice my silhouetted figure against the yellow dawn sky.

I stopped thinking and started climbing. Until, ten feet up, the pain from my torn hands forced me to let go and I banged my head against a ventilator as I fell awkwardly. For a few moments I lay there and stared unseeingly at the sky.

I actually cried a little with fear and frustration and shock. I wasn't very good at it, though. You need practice to be able to cry properly.

Then I started climbing again.

*

Somehow I got to the top. I don't even remember heaving myself over the narrow lip of the funnel rim, or the relief I must have felt when I found I had about ten inches of cover all around me, above the level of the rust and carbon scaled platform inside. I only know I lay there for what seemed an eternity while the pain from my bleeding, rope burned palms stabbed up my arms with monotonous agony.

Eventually I rolled over and opened my eyes. Oh Jesus! I slammed back with shock as I saw the huge, bulbous head rising above the forward rim of the funnel. In the dim light it was a monster beyond even my fevered imagination. Watching me with awful malignance as it clung to the steel lip which formed my limited horizon, immobile and threatening. . . .

I started to laugh.

Quietly at first. Then more and more uncontrollably, with the tears of near-hysteria trickling down my face. It was just the siren, the bloody *Ayacucho City*'s siren. Mounted on the funnel above the bridge. Where the gunmen still waited while the Liberian's crew were herded together from all over the ship. The gunmen . . . with guns.

God! I hooked my arm over the after end and felt wildly for the rope I'd just climbed. If I could do it, then a man with a pistol and a homicidally inquisitive disposition could, too. My fingers found it and I pulled until I'd recovered the bight, then I closed my eyes again and just lay there, listening to the gentle sigh of the wind in the foremast rigging and the slow purr of the auxiliary exhaust fumes as they puttered out of the carbonised hole of the stack.

The exhaust fumes? Hell, I'd forgotten all about them in my search for anonymity. Even now, with only the generator motors in operation below, I could already sense the acrid blue vapour contaminating the air about me. And when they started up the main engines . . .

I spat the sour taste of bile out of my throat. If? When? How? I'd had enough speculation in the past hour to satiate a hermit philosopher. I was alive, wasn't I . . . ? More or less . . . And, to coin a very worn old load of rubbish, where there's life there's . . . I tried to stop my backside waving in the air as I snaked around the black exhaust orifice towards the fore end. There was still life down there on the well deck but I didn't go much on the hope bit, certainly not for the poor bloody Greeks who didn't even know what it was all about.

Ever so cautiously I raised my head above the funnel lip, mentally thanking God for the supply of one ship's siren to break the otherwise clean outline. If I hadn't had that recently heart-stopping monstrosity there I knew I would never have dared to raise my eyes above my ten inch shield.

Yet, when I finally looked down on the still floodlit decks, I nearly screamed with mortification and deflated tension. I'd gone through sheer hell on earth to avoid detection. I'd even been astute enough to maroon myself on a carbon monoxide sun trap so that Clever Cable would avoid getting the deep six along with the less highly trained and intelligent members of the *Ayacucho City*'s crowd.

I suppose it was a natural consequence – me being the cutest. I mean, after all, I was the professional trouble shooter, the specialist in subterfuge and the techniques of self preservation, so I was bound to be the one to survive the longest.

Except that I was perched up here in the sky while, down below, they were letting the poor bloody useless Greeks go home.

And giving them a beautiful boat to do it with.

*

I felt my mouth sag open but I didn't bother closing it. It suited me better that way, like a drooling idiot's. It was almost full daylight now and I could see the details of the counterfeit H.M.S. *Diomede* quite clearly. I wondered irrelevantly how in God's name the high-jackers had ever got away with the whole crazy idea in the first place.

She was just an ordinary long-prowed fishing boat. Probably Sicilian by the lines of her. Roughly sixty feet long, beamy – and about as much like one of Her Majesty's Ships as a celluloid Mickey Mouse. Then I remembered the searchlight, and the way we'd been blinded by it for every minute of the hold-up, and I thought back to the Provost investigators' report on the Glen Dhearg job and the bit about the presumed reasons for the staged Volkswagen accident. It wasn't the first time the pirates had used dazzle for cover.

And it's surprising how a sixty foot drifter can sound exactly like a one hundred and fifty foot warship. Especially when you can't see it.

Only that wasn't the part that was upsetting me quite as much as the way the *Ayacucho City*'s late crew-men were being shepherded down the swaying pilot ladder and aboard the fisherman. Even the wounded foc'slehead look-out was there, being carefully lowered in a Robinson Stretcher by two gun-slung bluejackets to his Greek oppo's below.

I wasn't witnessing a mass murder. I was watching a highly civilised and inexplicable repatriation. And I wanted to be sick again.

Oh, not that I grudged the Greeks their good fortune. It was just that I knew I didn't have the guts – even with the evidence of humane treatment in front of me – to evacuate my bolt hole in the funnel and expose myself to the two dark skinned sailors on the bridge deck just below me, who still held their machine pistols in a very professional way to cover the activity on the foredeck.

So I just stayed where I was and watched as the leader of the boarders, still in the uniform of a Royal Naval lieutenant commander, leaned over the bridge front and shouted to Chief Officer Kanellopoulos as he swung his leg over the bulwarks – the last man of her original crew to leave the *Ayacucho City*.

'First Officer! Do you speak English?'

The Greek hesitated warily. I knew just how he felt, I was trying to figure it out too. 'A leetle . . . what you want?'

The new master of the Liberian gestured aft. 'I would suggest you make for Sicily, Mister. Your heading is three one five magnetic. Do you understand?'

Kanellopoulos looked down at the silent ranks of upturned faces on the heaving deck below. I hoped to God he wasn't going to do anything silly, the only time to protest now was from behind the open sights of a 4.7 naval gun. Then he shrugged and quickly climbed down the ladder where he was clutched aboard by eager hands.

I was conscious of the pent-up breath whistling between my teeth as the little stack of the fishing boat burst into a frenzied pop-popping and, with the Greeks still standing, silently accusing along her crowded decks, she sheered away from the slab sides of the freighter.

The men on the bridge watched unmoving until the trawler had settled on her reciprocal course back towards the distant mainland, then the Lieutenant Commander nodded his head to one of the gunmen. They both moved into the wheelhouse and for the first time I got a proper look at the face of the man who had pirated the *Ayacucho City*.

It was a dark, impassively handsome face. The face of the almost legendary heroes, straight from the pages of the Arabian Nights.

And I was sure, then, that I was looking at a one time up and coming officer of the Egyptian Navy – a man called Kamal Abul Hosni, also lately First Mate of the Dundee-bound merchantman *Farafra*. And probably also the man who had killed a lot of British soldiers in a place called Glen Dhearg.

And the man who intended to kill a lot more people, in a place called Israel.

The clang of the bridge telegraphs was answered immediately by the new Arab engineers below. Then I was coughing and retching in the lung-choking diesel exhaust fumes as the *Ayacucho City* slowly gathered way.

But it was far too late for me to do anything.

Except suffocate.

*

I nearly died in those next few minutes. Until the increasing wind of our passage as we worked up to seventeen knots formed a vacuum on the lee side of the funnel and sucked a large percentage of the waste gases away from my gasping mouth. Eventually I managed to achieve an unhappy combination of lying on my back and twisting my head far enough upward to allow my face to catch the blessedly cool stream of air.

But even during those long, long moments of near respiratory failure I knew I couldn't stay in that strained and deformed posture for more than a few hours. It was almost unendurable. Unless you happened to be dead.

I realised that could easily be arranged too, if I felt like a change.

Suddenly I had an idea. Carefully I risked a quick glance aft, down along the line of our wake. Yes, there she was – the fishing boat with her prize crew of forty-odd Greek survivors. If I could somehow let them know there was still someone aboard other than the violent people down below, maybe it would encourage the Authorities not only to act quicker to stop the *Ayacucho City*, but also to act rather more discreetly than if they thought she was just a shipload of piratical desperadoes.

Like dropping a stick of United Nations thousand pound bombs right down the bloody funnel I sat in.

Sat in? Sat *on* . . . ? Ah, what the hell . . . either way I was stuck up here like a daffodil in a poisoned flower pot. Slowly I raised my left wrist above the lip and tried to angle my watch face to catch the rays of the sun now well above the eastern horizon. Heliograph, that was it.

Like the old time navy used to do. Like Super Spy undoubtedly would do in my position – except that he would have had a five foot by five collapsible, self-illuminating one in his waistcoat pocket – and all Cable had was an inch and a quarter diameter Timex.

I tried to think about Robert the Bruce, and how he succeeded in the end. I also did my damnedest *not* to think about what would happen if all the Greeks on that boat were only half as blind as Third Mate Mikkos. I guessed he probably wouldn't even notice if I fired a Brock's benefit of multi-coloured distress rockets.

After I'd flashed in a frantic imitation of the Eddy-stone Light for a good five minutes I risked a second, surreptitious peep aft. She was still out there, now a good fifteen cables away and going like stink for Sicily. I could even make out the little black figures of the sailors crowding round the tiny wheelhouse on her deck.

Lucky, lucky bastards.

I flicked for another three minutes roughly.

Until she blew up.

*

I suppose it made sense. In fact, subconsciously, I think that was what prevented me from electing to join the Sicilian liberty boat. You see, I just couldn't figure out why Hosni could be so stupid as to free forty-odd blabbermouth Greeks when he must have known that First Mate Grigorios Kanellopoulos would make a visit to the local carabinieri H.Q. his number one priority.

I mean, when you intend to decimate a whole nation, why get all puritanical about over-killing a few dozen more? Especially when they could shop you before you even got to the killing ground.

No. Hosni could only afford one criterion – Think Big. And why not take the chance to dispose of the phoney British warship as well, all in the one economy-sized bang?

So I just watched, and clenched my fists helplessly, and maybe cried a little for the second time that day, while the time bombs planted in the fishing boat erupted in a great mushroom of dirty yellow water and shattered planks, and little bits of sailormen.

Then the dull boom of the explosion rumbled across the water, chasing us with tiny ripples of surface concussion until the atomised spray cleared under the stray caress of a sudden catspaw of wind, and I was blinking dully at the circle of miniature fountains as the debris splashed sullenly seawards again.

Suddenly it was very quiet.

And the sea astern was very, very empty.

I felt the anger choking me as I twisted my head to watch them down on the bridge deck. Christ, but they must be bloody delighted at the way everything was going for them. I bet there was even a smile on the bloody inscrutable face of the Sphinx!

But then I saw Hosni below me, and I didn't even have the satisfaction of hate to buoy me up.

He stood there, staring aft, and only the white grip of the clenched hands on the bridge rail indicated he had any feelings at all. And beside him stood the girl, Fathi. I watched as the two stayed immobile even after the last whisp of smoke had cleared over our wake and, all the time, I was haunted by that strange lost, sad look on the girl's face and the curiously pathetic intimacy between them.

And I sank back in my carbon flower pot staring unseeingly at the sky. Go on, please gloat, you bastards. Let Cable get a good hate worked up so at least he'd have the satisfaction of choking up here with all the dignity of a martyred crusader under the swords of the evil ... Oh, why the hell did they have to be so like ordinary people? For anyone to do what they were doing they should be incapable of tenderness, or sorrow or any of the other emotions felt by us mediocre, unpatriotic human beings.

It complicated things too much for me. Even with the knowledge of what the *Ayacucho City* carried, it spoilt my crusader image and left me feeling like just another bloody do-gooder in someone else's war.

It also made it that much harder to work out ways of stopping this shipload of horror.

Like killing the man and the girl below me.

*

I lay up there on top of that bloody funnel for maybe two million years, alternating between unconsciousness and a hazy twilight of lung-racking delirium. Then I looked at my Timex and found it was only 10 a.m. – four bells in the forenoon watch – and rolled over as the muscles of my straining neck and shoulder knotted in an agony of cramp.

The seizure passed, leaving me gasping harder than before and also increasingly aware of the yellow ball cf the Mediterranean sun as the growing heat from it gradually turned the steel plates I was lying on into a giant, economy-sized frying pan. With me as the dinner.

And I was thirsty. Desperately, uncontrollably thirsty.

I twisted round cautiously. There was at least another twelve hours of this dehydrating misery to be endured before I could even consider venturing down my private halyard to the exposed decks below. And once down I was liable to get a more permanent cure for thirst than a glass of water. It wasn't a bundle of fun being a hero – especially a reluctant one.

Something twinkled momentarily on the other side of the funnel. Water? I couldn't be that lucky, just as likely to be a handful of diamonds up here in chimney land. . . . I wriggled painfully round the belching exhaust pipe, hoping to Christ it *wasn't* diamonds. It's funny how your sense of values changes with your environment. For instance, right then I would have been happier with the feel of a .45 Colt Peacemaker in my hand than any dolly girl's. . . .

I stared down at the tiny pool of water and wanted to cry again. Water! All I'd found was a film of liquid rust trapped in the carbonised hollow of a stopped-up drain. I started to swear softly and repetitively under my breath as I watched the shimmering vibrations from the engines churn the precious liquid into a permanently blood red cloud.

Running out of words that were both filthy and vicious enough to suit the occasion I started all over again just for kicks. Then I dabbed my hankie carefully into the mess until it was the colour of a used field dressing and held it to my cracked lips. It felt cool against my flushed skin but the strain of keeping it out of my limekiln mouth made me thirstier than ever.

I flopped over on my back again and spent the next few minutes of suffocating time thinking about that farm I was going to have if I ever got out of this bloody B.M.S.N.C. shambles, and about the cows and the sheep in the fields, and the hens . . . no, I wasn't going to have any hens. I mean, they're O.K. when they're all little and fluffy like Easter chicks, but they get bigger and develop nasty, cold beady eyes that stare right through you. . . . And the ducks. I'd keep a few ducks, maybe. On the pond. Sitting in the water.

In the water. The bloody, bloody water . . . Jesus, I wish I was dead.

Then there was a sudden noise from forr'ad, and I got sick with fright in case someone had heard me and was going to oblige with a 7.62 mm. Russian shell at the base of my lying skull.

For a few moments I froze there, watching as the masts swayed gently above me and listening to the oddly familiar sound. Then I realised what it was and half crawled, half scrambled for the cover of the siren casing as the slowly turning cargo winches on the forward well deck chattered into more urgent life and, above the lip of the funnel, I saw the topping lifts of number one hatch derricks take the strain.

They were preparing to remove the hatch covers and expose the grain in the *Ayacucho City*'s holds.

Which could only mean one thing.

They were going to release Anthrax-B.

*

Kamal Abul Hosni was a good officer. At least, he seemed to do a lot of the things that a good officer should, like leading by example and not from the rear as seemed to be the strategy of a great many of his Egyptian contemporaries.

Or maybe that was just a vicious rumour put out by a biased Israeli propaganda agency. Along with fake newsreel shots of Egyptian tanks, guns and boots left behind in the Sinai Desert.

Either way, Hosni was preparing to handle the killer bacilli himself, though I had a nasty feeling that if anything went wrong the *Ayacucho City* would run out of sea room at the eastern end of the Med and keep on ploughing right across the Holy Land, because there would be no one left alive aboard to stop her.

Including Daffodil Cable up here.

The girl appeared from under the break of the centrecastle accompanied by two Arab sailors carrying something white. They spread it out on the steel deck beside the gaping number one hold and I saw it was one of the engine room asbestos fire suits. I thought how appropriate it looked, splayed out like a drawn corpse. Except that anthrax cadavers were black, the black of corruption, and the empty, sightless eyes of the dead.

A few minutes later the girl slipped the huge, plexiglass visored helmet over Hosni's shoulders and stood back. The current master of the Liberian was uniformed for war, 1970's style. I smiled sardonically through the brackets of the siren. He was bloody dressed, all right – dressed to kill.

Then another Arab very carefully carried a small black briefcase with shiny brass locks along the deck and placed it beside an already prepared bucket of what I took to be water. I recognised the case, I'd read its description often enough, and the bucket contained the required dilutant as specified in Ministry of Defence (Chemical and Bacteriological Warfare Department) Operations Manual 9868/342 BW, section 84, paras. 12 et seq.

Someone else produced a gleaming brass syringe like the ones you use to spray weed killer on the garden path and they were ready. The Jordanian girl hesitated a moment in front of Hosni, then abruptly turned and walked aft towards the centrecastle while the ungainly, monstrous figure raised a hand to the men on the bridge.

I squinted down to see the watchkeeper wave back, then half turn towards the wheelhouse and issue a sharp order in guttural Arabic. Immediately the jangle of the engine room telegraphs broke the soft throb of the huge diesels, then the throb itself cut dead and we coasted along through the glassy calm with only the whisper of the waves to acknowledge our existence.

I dragged great gouts of wonderfully clean air into my tortured lungs as the jetting exhaust dwindled to a rumbling trickle. Somehow the world seemed a much nicer place for those very few minutes and I was grateful for the caution that made Hosni stop the ship to minimise the danger of contamination caused by the wind of our passage.

Then the way was off the ship completely and we lay dead in the water, with the hot sun burning down on the back of my neck and the steel bowl of the funnel getting hotter and hotter. I began to wonder whether suffocating wasn't preferable to grilling.

Until Hosni bent down on one knee and lifted the flask out of its case with infinite care, and I forgot all about the heat and the thirst and the discomfort, and watched a man preparing to commit history's biggest crime against the Human Race.

A movement on the bridge deck. The girl climbed the starboard ladder and quietly moved across to the dodgers beside the dark skinned men. Then we all gazed in silent awe as Kamal Abul Hosni unscrewed the stopper from the flask and gently, ever so gently, poured a hundred million agonising deaths into the bright galvanised bucket.

He stood up slowly with the syringe in misshapen gloved hands and, filling it, moved clumsily over to the forward end of number one. They'd left the hatch beams in position to form a steel web over the open square. Hosni clambered up over the chipped hatch coaming and stood erect on the end of the first beam. Below him the grain looked warm and yellow in the brilliant sunlight yet I still shivered, remembering the way I'd nearly drowned in its soft clutches.

Then he was leaning slightly forward, with the brass cylinder held out before him, and I saw the white clad arm pump carefully forward while the fine spray twinkled prettily in the sun as a tiny rainbow of horror hissed over the golden carpet below.

A little rivulet of sweat ran down my nose and splashed on the back of my wrist. I licked it off unthinkingly, then pulled a face as the bitter saltiness hit my palate. Christ but I could do with a long drink of water, cold as the condensation on a whore's heart. . . . I looked out towards the *Ayacucho City*'s bows again and saw that Hosni had moved right along the transverse beam, then the ungainly, frightened figure stepped clumsily down to the lip of the coaming and, moving gingerly aft, slowly sprayed the whole surface of the cargo in number one hold.

He beckoned to the watchers and warily they moved forward towards the hatch. There were fourteen men on the foredeck altogether so it appeared that there had been more waiting to board from the fishing boat, probably the least English looking. I guessed that, including the two watchkeepers on the bridge and, say, another two down below on the control platform, I now had a minimum of eighteen very tough boys to contend with. Plus the girl, Fathi, of course.

Mind you, I was British, dammit. Which made all the difference.

I was also a coward. That brought the odds back to nineteen to one again.

The winches started to rattle and the first hatch board jerked into the air, swinging over the contaminated hold. Two men, moving very carefully, guided it into place and gradually the virulent square was covered over. Leaving one group to batten down and wedge the tarpaulin the rest of the crowd moved aft and, with Hosni standing in isolated quarantine under the break of the foc'sle, number two was quickly broached.

I watched for the next hour in thoughtful silence until all three forward holds had been adulterated then, as the deck gang followed Hosni from my field of vision to tackle the after decks, I rolled over and drifted off into a fitful, nightmare sleep in which I was frying in a huge pan while all the time the ghoulish figure of Hosni – asbestos clad but with a British naval rating's cap – poked me with a shiny brass toasting fork . . . and in the background a black bearded Captain Constantine Argenti planted blood red daffodils in the bullet holes in his chest, and laughingly roared that 'next I, Argenti, will bluddy love up Mistra Cabel, hah' . . . until J.C. and McReadie rowed past in a little plastic destroyer and J.C. stood up waving a Lion Passant flag and shouted 'Shoot! Shoot! SHOOT!' . . . while McReadie fired a garden syringe into the frying pan . . . and I looked down and saw it was a glass bottle containing a piece of a man's lung . . . and the cap of the bottle broke off and black diesel fumes started to envelope the sliver of lung as it rose and fell and rose and fell . . .

. . . and I was gasping for oxygen while I slammed back into the present as the telegraphs jangled below me and the gaping maw of the exhaust roared into life.

Then I was whimpering with the returning shock of it all, and clawing for the stream of air curling over the funnel lip as the Liberian's bow swung round and she steadied on a heading for the Port of Haifa.

The time was 4.20 p.m. It had taken precisely six hours to turn the *Ayacucho City* from an innocuous ocean going freighter into the most lethal, obscene weapon in the world.

And I had another six hours of this bloody un-endurable torment before I even dared to move.

I was sick again. But only in a dry, gagging sort of way.

*

I tied the last knot in the halyard and sat back, allowing the wind to play over my parched lips and the square inches of sun frizzled tissue that was my face. Whatever happened, I had to move. Evacuate this bloody awful trap before the sun rose again and drove me out of what little was left of my mind.

I was a dead man anyway, stay or go. I knew what I had to do, and I also knew that they would kill me before I even got to first base. But there was something inside me – not courage, oh Jesus, no – more a kind of frustrated anger at being so bloody ineffectual and frightened, preferring to skulk towards a miserable little private death up here instead of doing something, anything, to hit back at those misguided bastards down there who were trying to set the whole bloody world on fire.

It was my world too, and I liked it just the way it was.

So I was going to try and keep it like that. As my legacy. By sinking this goddamned ship.

I glanced at the luminous glow from my watch – 11.17. I had been up here for nearly twenty-four hours, and I hadn't enjoyed it one bit. I dropped the coil of knotted halyard over the lip of the funnel and swung my leg over after it. The cramp hit me again, though, and I sort of flopped forward on to my face in the little puddle of dissolved rust. Eventually the pains subsided slightly and I swore for the hundredth time at B.M.S.N.C. and Hosni and the Jews and the Arabs, and at all the evil, scientific harlots who'd produced Anthrax-B in the first place.

Then I lifted my other leg laboriously into space and just hung there, bent over the top of the funnel and feeling a right bloody idiot. Because I didn't know what to do next, what with my arms feeling like tubes of jelly and not having the strength to take the weight of my suspended body once my armpits lost their hook over the edge.

It seemed like an eternity before my flailing legs managed to find the first knot in the halyard and I was

F   161 able to take the strain with my feet, only seconds, apparently, before my arms popped from their sockets and I plumeted through the eighty feet to the engine beds, via skylight junction.

Finally I let go of the lip and froze for a few moments, watching the bridge wing for the first signs of a man with a machine gun and a curious mind to appear. Surely the watchkeepers had heard me threshing around up here in the air? And my body must be silhouetted against the starry night sky like a black paper warlock.

But a couple of decades dragged past and nobody came out of the wheelhouse so I closed my eyes in relief for another few moments before sliding painfully and shakily to the deck.

I managed to scramble away from the cone of light around the skylight, then just lay and panted and hugged my torn hands under my bruised armpits and prayed to God for another few minutes of that precious luck I needed so much.

No one there. It felt uncanny with the only sounds from the constant rumble of the engines and the sighing of the undulating waves along our racing hull. I could tell by the excessive vibration in the deck that we were really steaming hard, but then Hosni was clever, clever enough to realise that the *Ayacucho City* had to make up for the period when she was stopped. There couldn't be any time gap to excite suspicion, to promote awkward questions about why we were so far past our E.T.A. Haifa.

I also wondered briefly how on earth he ever expected to get away with impersonating the late Captain Argenti when he did arrive, but then why should anyone have any possible reason to doubt that the man on a ship's bridge with the four gold bars on his shoulder wasn't her master? And anyway, for a bloke who could turn a wooden trawler into a warship with only a scrap of uniform and a thousand watt bulb, the problem didn't even exist.

I took a deep breath, climbed down the vertical ladder beside the wrecked W.T. cabin, and scuttled furtively aft along the boat deck until I merged into the shadows under the stern of number three lifeboat. Above my head the black painted letters stood out against the white of the planking – AYACUCHO CITY. MONROVIA.

I grinned without a lot of humour. Monrovia. It sounded like somewhere out of a Gilbert and Sullivan opera. Or an adventure book for boys.

Except that in those stories the hero never got killed. And I seemed hell-bent on spoiling the bloody tradition.

The nervous tic was dragging at the corner of my mouth as I peered cautiously forward towards the silhouetted line of the bridge. No sign of movement there. I bit my lip savagely, starting to get irritated at my lack of muscular control then, keeping low, flitted to the top of the ladder leading down to the promenade deck.

Half-way down. Those damned deckhead lights seem very bright.

Oh *Christ!* Footsteps. Coming towards me ... up the next stairway from the lower deck ...

... I turned and desperately scrambled back up, virtually throwing myself full length under the shadowy bulk of the boat I'd just left, conscious at the same time of the blinding starfish of pain as my forehead struck the handle of the davit winch.

I stopped breathing again, voluntarily this time, as the man pulled himself up to the boatdeck and turned forward towards the bridge. I caught a worm's eye view of his face as he passed – dark skinned and hawkish, with the eyes dulled by the remnants of sleep like any other seaman on his way to take over the graveyard watch.

My mouth started twitching again. I didn't like the implications in the traditional description of the midnight to four duty spell.

I saw the man was now dressed in ordinary jeans and a sweater. Without the Navy rig he didn't look at all British. And neither did the Russian Decteriov machine gun slung casually over his shoulder. It had occurred to me that I might have been able to place their unit's country of origin by the weapons they carried, but this crowd had the most cosmopolitan assortment of portable killing gear I'd ever seen in my life – Soviet, U.S., Czech, the good old British Sten and its current oppo, the Sterling, and at least one man with the new Cuban manufactured Che Guevara machine pistol.

More like a second hand gunsmiths than an assault commando.

Though personally it was a matter of complete indifference whether the bullet that finally eviscerated me sported a red star, a Chinese dragon or a Union bloody Jack.

The next time I hit the stairway I went down as though I was walking on land mines.

The prom deck alleyway was deserted this time. Flattening into the recessed entrance to the passenger accommodation I peered round the corner to the next ladder well. I had to get down that one too before I could attempt phase two of Operation Bath Plug. Except that I figured on letting the water *in*, not out.

I'd screwed up enough courage to go again when I hesitated. My cabin was less than twenty feet away, along the internal passage. And there was a washbasin in it. And washbasins had taps. With water. I touched my swollen lips with the tip of my dehydrated tongue ... dare I? In fact, *should* I? Wasn't it the kind of unnecessary risk only an irresponsibly selfish bastard with no thought for others would take?

The irresponsible, selfish bastard stuck his head into the corridor and blinked in the glare of the un-accustomed lights. So who needed night vision anyway? A blind paralytic with a wooden leg had as much chance of making it down thirty feet of brilliantly lit open steel ladders to the engine control platform, and disposing of a minimum of two large Arabian commandos armed with submachine guns and grenades, and knives. And bloody great fists. . . .

I shuddered involuntarily. It wasn't Super Spy I

needed for this job, it was the Royal Marines. And even if I did all that *and* managed to smash the intake valves down in the *Ayacucho City*'s belly I still had to get back up those near vertical ladders before the ship lay over on top of me, and all the time maybe with a lot of very disappointed, unchuffed pirates shooting things. Like bullets. . . .

I threw myself across the passage towards my cabin door, not caring very much whether any casual nocturnal wanderer saw me or not from the open door of the passenger lounge forr'ad. If they didn't, then I'd at least get the water I'd been dreaming about for the past twenty-four tormented hours. And if they did – I wouldn't need it.

Nobody shot me on the way across and, when I entered with a surge of relief at the door being un-locked, the cabin was empty and still. Shakily I closed the slatted door behind me and leaned back against it with the sweat pouring down my face and my whole body trembling with fear.

Christ, but my nerves were shot to hell. I'd never felt so utterly terrified in my life. A little voice kept screaming at the back of my mind, 'Don't be a silly sod, Cable boy. Get back up to your private chimney house an' the hell with being a fuggin' hero . . . !'

Then the voice faltered and the cabin grew hazy, and I saw a vision of a little Jewish kiddy – or was it an Arab? – with a trusting, happy smile and those bloody great Santa Claus is coming eyes, holding out its hand for a loaf of bread. But the bread was all black and

166

suppurating with disease inside, while Cable was alive and well and living in the top of a yellow painted funnel. . . .

Lurching towards the carafe of wonderful crystal liquid in the rack over the basin, I just stood there with the water running down my chin, soaking into my shirt with delightful coolness, while my throat muscles worked spasmodically to swallow and swallow and swallow.

Refilling the carafe with nervous hands, I drank another nectarine half and allowed the rest to upturn over my head until the hair was plastered down over my brow. Then I found myself grinning foolishly at the image in the mirror which must have been me, though it looked more like a Brylcreemed wooden Indian with the varnish peeling off, and thinking 'Jesus, Cable boy. You were ugly enough before but . . .'

Taking a deep breath I sucked my belly in and felt rugged – apart from the headache, the muscular spasms, the strained arms and the slowly growing stomach pains from the sudden excess of water. And the fact that I knew that, if I didn't go right now, I'd just curl up in a corner and start to cry with the paralysing fear which still gripped me.

I moved towards the door, then hesitated. Whether or not they'd fallen for my earlier mock-suicide, they'd also searched the cabin, that was obvious from the way my gear was strewn about all over the floor and my empty, upturned suitcase on the bunk. I scarcely even bothered to look for the gun I'd left on top of the wardrobe – Robin and his Arabian hoods up there were too efficient, too professional – but I'd caught sight of a little yellow cylinder projecting from under the bunk. I picked it up and toyed with it thoughtfully.

The container. The second one they'd supplied me with back in London. They'd given me two sample canisters just in case of a circuit malfunction. The first I'd flung over the side as instructed, that time we passed through the Gibraltar Straits. But the Navy had been expecting that one, waiting for it ... I shrugged. I couldn't see any real use for it but I tucked the spare into my belt as I eased the cabin door open and stepped out into the still deserted corridor.

I estimated I had about another six minutes to live. Give or take an eternity or two.

*

The starboard door to the engine room was open, hooked back against the bulkhead, and I hugged the shadow of a ventilator as I listened to the rush of the sea twenty feet below, only faintly discernible above the throbbing roar of the diesels. I closed my eyes as the fear swamped over me again, knotting and icing in my belly, then moved forward into the shaft of searching light shining out across the alleyway.

The first thing I was conscious of as I stepped on to the chequered steel plating at the top of the gleaming, grease-filmed ladders, was the noise. It never ceased to astonish me how ships' engineers could accustom themselves to working for hours in an atmosphere where the roar and the heat and the oil-laden air virtually over-powered you in an enveloping, treacly over-kill of sensation.

But I didn't mind it this time, not one bit. I could have gone down those ladders singing 'Land of Hope and Glory' to the massed bands of the Salvation Army and no one would have heard.

Though I'd have preferred the massed machine guns of the British Army right then.

I apprehensively stuck my head over the rail and looked down past the maze of red, blue and green painted asbestos-lagged pipes to where the *Ayacucho City*'s engine control platform should have been situated. And it was. About thirty feet below me and directly underneath.

And there was a white-overalled man sitting at the watchkeeper's desk, leaning well back in his chair with his hands behind his head and looking very bored.

But he only needed five seconds to stop looking bored and pull the trigger of the L2A3 Sterling which lay casually across the late Greek Chief's fuel log on the desk.

Directly underneath me. . . . I cast around hopefully for something to drop on him to distract his attention. Like a steel bench or the spare anchor. But there was nothing moveable up here in this sterile maze of tubing. Twisting up my face into a grimace of disgust I gazed past the control platform to the engine bed plates even further down. Somewhere amongst that bewildering mass of machinery were the ship's valves and sea water cooling inlets, maybe even her seacocks which, when opened or smashed, would flood the *Ayacucho City*'s engine space and sink her despite all Hosni's dedicated killing.

But to get that far meant I had to pass the duty engineer, and I wasn't convinced yet that he was the only one on watch down here. There must be at least two of them, probably one acting as greaser and general dog's body, but where? Where the blazes could he be working?

I started down the first run of ladder trying to look in every direction at once. After four or five treads I had to stop to shake the sweat out of my eyes. God, but it was as hot and humid as Judgement Day; but then, maybe it was?

Glancing down, I felt a little better when I realised that, until I turned the 180 degree angle at the next landing, the Arab at the controls couldn't see me anymore. Now the depth of the steel treads obscured me from his view even if he did have cause to glance directly above his head.

Where in God's name *is* that other bloody watch-keeper?

Quickly down to the landing. Easy, Cable boy, the dodgy bit next ... less than twenty feet above the control panel now and I was going to have to about turn down the next flight – where the engineer with the Sterling only had to lean back a bit further, look up casually, and ...

I bit my lip viciously to stop the twitching. Go *on,*

you heroic, stupid bastard! One tread. Two . . . only ten more to go. Three, four, five . . . Jeeeeeze, the wog's goin' to turn roun . . . No! Just stretching. My God but I'm bloody thirsty again. Six treads . . . seven . . . You're there, Mister. You're nearly there . . . Eight, nine and te . . . '

And I found the second watchkeeper.

About three feet in front of me.

Christ!

*

He was tall, dark and thin – I didn't wait to see anymore. But he was every bit as shattered by the sudden confrontation as I was. No wonder I'd not been able to see him before, he was actually coming up the ladder while I was going down. Cable's luck had definitely expired. Along with my heroic intentions.

We stood there staring at each other for what seemed like a very long time, the Arab with his mouth gaping wider and wider like an expanding pink hole in a leather hide, and me with nerves twanging hysterically.

Then he screamed something which sounded like 'Holy fuggin' Mahomet, Abdul!' but was probably a bit more Arabic than that, and I saw the gunman at the desk slamming erect, grabbing for the gun and swinging round towards us all in one smooth, reflex action.

There comes a time when every man should admit defeat, and I'd just heard the clock chiming for me. It was also the time when I was scheduled to attack with the swift, deadly karate blows of the highly trained B.M.S.N.C. operator. But I didn't.

All I actually managed to do was to lash out with one panic-stricken foot. Hosni's man doubled up, clutching his groin in agony, while I stared wide-eyed at him, conscious of a faint stirring of surprised pride underneath the terror. Then he folded over the shiny rail and hung there like a sack of sawdust. I'd half bent to grab his feet and tip him over on to the smoking cylinder head of the starboard engine before I became aware of the snick of a Sterling bolt smacking into the 'Fire' position.

It was pretty sharp of me to figure the next move. I drew a mental line between the gunman on the platform and my only escape route via the ladder I'd just descended . . . and my retired oppo was beautifully balanced right in the line of fire. Which meant his mate down below would have to waste vital seconds in changing his aiming point.

It's funny how your mind can suddenly slam into top gear under pressure, and your actions are dictated, not by fear anymore, but by a crystal clear, all-anticipating brain. And that's the way I felt as I literally glided back up the first four treads of the ladder in a superbly smooth ripple of pure muscular beauty.

Until – on tread number five – it all went wrong when the bastard in the white suit started firing *through*, instead of round, his sagging mate.

And my intoxicating ripple mutated into a frantic,

clawing scramble as I felt the white hot shells spang into the steel rails on either side of me.

Dimly I was aware of a crumpled corpse, still bent in the middle, jerking and jumping and cavorting obscenely while the 9 mm. short bursts literally tore it to pieces. Then someone was screaming in sheer terror and I realised it was me, and it made me remember the hate and shock in Constantine Argenti's voice when he was driven back and back and over and down into the cold black sea below . . .

. . . then, somehow, I had stumbled round the angle of the ladder to see, still horrifyingly high above me, the rectangle of the engine room doorway. The staccato chatter of the submachine gun finally hesitated and I heard, above the pounding, overwhelming roar of the machinery, an empty magazine hit the deck.

And the smack of a new one being driven home with the dexterity of a professional killer.

*

I was still less than half-way up the gleaming path to safety, even then only vaguely registering that I was up against men so calculating that they would gun down one of their own crowd in cold blood before jeopardizing the success of their mission, when I found out just how calculating they could be.

As, instead of a fruitless chase up the ladder after my fast disappearing backside, the gunman on the platform below fired very deliberate bursts at point blank range into the thin steel treads under my feet.

A Plague of Sailors

The first four or five rounds smashed into the treads slightly higher than the one I was on. I stopped, petrified with the shock of not knowing what was happening while the narrow, diamond-etched steel plate under my eyes suddenly clanged shatteringly and a row of huge, shiny blisters erupted in a haze of glittering, supersonic metal flakes.

Clasping my hands to my face in agony as the super-heated steel shards sliced long bleeding runnels in a fan from my chin to my cheek bones, I took one involuntary step back. Then the second burst pounded into the very tread my lower foot rested upon.

It was like being kicked by a steam hammer. Repeatedly.

And it only needed one shell to penetrate right through. . . .

Ironically I think it was the impetus from the ensuing bursts of fire which actually drove me, leaping and skipping like an uncontrollable crazyman, right up to the top of those distorting, bullet-pocked ladders.

Even the platform at the doorway spangled into a web of shimmering bubbles under the relentless hosing of the inverted Sterling. I had to keep on my feet ... Christ, if I went down, even on one knee, the impact would shatter my shin and thigh bones like sugar sticks ... I hurled myself across the raised coaming and out into the dark starboard alley, still with eyes bulging and mouth gaping in the last whisper of my shrieking terror.

I don't really remember my actions from then on.

I only have a nightmare image of running, running God only knows where. Forward or aft? I don't know. I just retain the agony of my pounding legs as I struggled for the blessed safety of the anonymous darkness at the end of the *Ayacucho City*'s centrecastle.

And then even the goddamned night itself turned Judas on me as the clamour of more automatic fire blasted in my face. I had one brief glimpse of straddle-legged figures silhouetted behind the stabbing muzzle flashes . . . and the white painted bulkheads around me were screeching with an eternity of ricochets . . . then I was sobbing hysterically as I just kept on running up and along the black line of the bulwarks. And out . . . and down. . . .

Dearest Mother . . . Please to God, help meeeeeee!

Until the icy mountains of the sea crashed over me, and dragged me further and further into the bottomless hell where the fishes nibble at the fingers of dead men.

And I started to drown.

Chapter Five

I surfaced eventually.

It seemed like the next day, but I don't really think it could have been because, when my lungs finally started to pump air again, the great moving cliff that was the *Ayacucho City* was still gliding past me. Except that, instead of a gentle whisper, the sound of her passage was now a smashing, rumbling crescendo of force with the beating whup . . . whup . . . whup of her huge propellers steadily increasing in volume as . . .

Her propellers! Those bloody enormous, spinning phosphor-bronze cleavers. And she was a twin screw ship . . . with the starboard screw almost certainly right handed, dragging the surface layers down, under, and in . . . along with anything that floated. And I'd gone over the wall on her starboard side. . . .

A terrified glimpse of the white load line markings passing over me like ghostly fingers, then the sea spun me round and I cartwheeled back under in a crazy, slow motion spiral with my ears roaring and the bubbles streaming from my cod fish mouth.

Then I was up again with the black steel slab a greater distance from me now, but it wasn't because I'd moved further out from her sides, it was because the hull form was fining down towards her stern.

176

Getting more and more slender as the overhanging counter ploughed towards where I was choking. And under the counter was the rudder, and the threshing screws.

Whup . . . ! Whup . . . ! Whup . . . !

I tried to fling myself bodily backwards in the water, arms flailing in blind panic, but it was no bloody good. It was like an iron filing trying to avoid an electromagnet. The suction plucked at me and I felt myself going, dragging down, down, down, deeper and deeper, with the hair trailing out behind me in wriggling tentacles and eyes bulging under the increasing pressure.

Then I was below the ship itself, suspended on my belly like a free-fall parachutist with my legs bent up towards the sky I'd never know again, and the steel blanket of the hull sliding above me . . . and it was as quiet as the inside of a dead man's chest, because the crash of the sea didn't exist down here in the sleeping place of all the poor drowned sailormen . . . except for the beating. The bloody beating of those great, churning . . .

Oh my Christ! I could see them. I could actually *see* them through the blackness, gliding towards me like spectral windmills, each encased in a rifled vortex of a hundred million tiny luminescent bubbles . . . and it was very interesting, and pretty . . . and so quiet. So wonderfully quiet.

Except for the beating.

Whup! Whup! Whup! W H U P . . . W H U . . . !

177

And then they stopped turning. Just like that.

Like switching the light out. And all the little bubbles were switched off too, one after the other, chasing and twinkling and spiralling off up to Heaven. I was very disappointed . . . because it was terribly cold without the light . . . I was so sad I wanted to cry . . .

. . . then something that must have been a slab of phosphor-bronze sneaked out of the submarine night and hit me a seventeen knot blow on the shoulder.

*

Finally the bubbles switched back on again, sparkling and winking, until I realised they weren't bubbles any more – they were the stars in the blue-black sky.

I stared foolishly at them for a moment, still swirling slowly on my now vertical axis in the surface currents of the *Ayacucho City*'s wake, until a little wavelet reared up in front of me, slapped me in the face, and I went down under again while my first deep, wonderful breath turned abruptly to a further rush of salt water into already battered lungs.

Then I came up, and went down.

And came up again and bloody went down.

And for a very long time I alternated between drowning and breathing until finally I got mad in a dazed sort of way and floundered desperately to stay on the surface while, all the time, that little voice kept shouting 'Stay down, you dumb bastard! Just go back down among the dead men. . . . You're one of them now anyway, Cable. One of the lost sailors ... 'cause you got a fuggin' lifetime of swimming ahead of you, an' that means two, maybe three, hours at the most. You're beat, Cable ... you haven't got the bloody strength to float 'til morning, never mind set course for Libya ... or Greece? ... or Crete? Jeeeze, where in God's name *are* you anyway ...? Apart from in the Mediterranean bloody Sea. ...'

Then I had a good retching cough, and a spit, and managed to tread water long enough to look around though most of the time all I could see were the tops of the waves sliding across the yellow disc of the moon above me.

There wasn't much of a sea running at all, really, but when your eyes are only inches above the surface of the water even a twelve inch ripple is like a tidal wave. I shook my head to clear the film from my eyes, then a slightly larger swell lifted me a bit higher and I saw her – the *Ayacucho City*.

She was lying about three cables away, long and black in the darkness with the only relief in the rows of lights along her centrecastle alleyways and the rectangle of an open door on her poop housing.

And the questing beam of her fourteen inch bridge searchlight as it stalked the wave crests.

Looking for me.

A cross wave smacked at me and I went under again while the pain from my injured shoulder clawed up the side of my skull. There was something else wrong too, something digging into my groin with steely insistent fingers. I broke surface and actually grinned a little wryly. What the hell, I was probably the only bloke afloat in the Med right this minute who'd been fried, dehydrated, drowned, shot at and bloody well run over by a ten thousand ton ship.

It wasn't much fun, but it did pass the day.

And those screws, churning towards me. I shuddered a little, just remembering, and imagining the eviscerated, shredded obscenity that might have been floating here in my place. Another few revolutions and ... I didn't want to think any more. Presumably either the homicidal engineer or the bridge watchkeeper had stopped her just before the *Ayacucho City* did a far better job of neutralising Brevet Cable than any submachine gun.

The wave lifted me again and I could see that she was now facing almost directly towards me, steaming at slow speed along a reciprocal course to try and pick me up in the beam of her goddamned searchlight. But it takes a long time to stop a ship from full speed, a good seven or eight lengths even with both screws churning full astern. That was the only thing that had saved me – that short period during the manoeuvre when the shafts were thrown from ahead to astern and the propellers were idle. Yet even then they'd hit me ... Super Spy your luck I don't need any more. Brevet Cable supplies his own.

Christ, but she's getting a bit close, though!

There wasn't anything I could do. Swimming away

would be like a slug trying to outpace a leopard, and they didn't really know where I was anyway. Apart from calculating the distance they'd overshot they also had to allow for the turning circle of the ship, and the drift, and the highly unlikely assumption that I was still alive in the first place.

The yellow lance stabbed into the sea less than a hundred feet from where I floated.

Of course it was impossible. They couldn't find me if they searched all night. I was a seaman, and I knew.

The waves sparkled brightly – only fifty feet away now. I brought my knees up and tried to kick feebly away but the pain in my guts niggled awkwardly so I gave up trying to avoid the inevitable.

Thirty feet. For a man attempting the impossible Hosni was having a bloody good try.

Twenty feet. I glimpsed my hand reflecting whitely in the water beside me. God, the bulk of the ship was filling my whole horizon now. They would see me. They *must* see me . . . the searchlight vectored another ten feet until I could have stretched out and grasped the edge of its beam.

I didn't even have the presence of mind to dive. I just lay there like a bloody marker buoy and closed my eyes, waiting for the smash of gunfire above me.

Suddenly the whole world blazed and my screwed-up eyelids turned an opaque red as the dazzle hit them squarely. The blinding glare burned into my sockets, and I wanted to shout 'Please. Please don't! Not after all that. . . .' Then the light had swept past me until at last it snapped out in the distance.

Like switching off a bubble. It was very disconcerting.

High above me the jangle of bridge telegraphs, then the muted echo from down below, and the pulse of the engines quickened. I opened my eyes and stared foolishly – surely to Christ they weren't going to try and run me down again. Not when a spray of nine millimetre farewells would do just as well, and with a lot less trouble.

I heard the sound of the screws beginning to thresh the water. Whup . . . whup . . . WHUP . . . and the terror swamped over me as the memories started to return.

Then the high bows fell away above me and her silhouette lengthened as she turned back towards Haifa, and I grinned like a bloody idiot and just paddled with my hands and watched the stern come round with the white water kicking high under her counter and, even in the near darkness, the still visible letters AYACUCHO CITY. MONROVIA.

I watched as she merged into the dark line of the eastern horizon. Until her stern light faded to a pinpoint, then vanished. I swallowed quite a few mouthfuls of sea water at the same time and knew I was going to be bloody thirsty very soon. I also started to feel lonely, which was quite ridiculous considering the alternative.

If they'd kept on searching for another millisecond.

Until the white blob of my face had time to register in the brain of the searchlight operator . . . but of course, I hadn't really been worried in case they'd found me. It was impossible.

I mean, I was a seaman. And I knew.

*

I started to swim to Libya.

Brevet Cable. Voyage One. Speed 0.005 knots. Cargo, a bellyful of sea water. Ship's call sign, H.E.L.P. Estimated time of arrival, two (2) weeks. Fug it!

I suddenly remembered the area of the Mediterranean was only 1,145,000 square miles and felt a bit better. For a nasty moment I'd thought it was much larger.

Hell, I even had a course and a star to steer me by. My heading was 180 degrees true, give or take a couple of points. I knew that because the *Ayacucho City* must have been disappearing approximately due east and I'd churned around through another 90 degrees to point me towards Africa.

I wish I knew what was wrong with my guts.

After ten minutes I couldn't stand it any longer. Every time I drew my legs up to kick out, the pressure in my groin increased. I started to get scared. Maybe I was ruptured internally? Or even split open? And I wasn't feeling the pain yet because of the analgesic effect of the cold water? Oh God in Heaven, maybe I was trailing a thin red coil of entrai . . . I turned on my back and, spitting and retching as the waves broke against the back of my head, placed trembling hands on my lower abdomen.

I wish I hadn't laughed.

I mean, it's a bit of a bizarre thing for a bloke to do when he's swimming in the middle of the night in the middle of the ocean. In the middle of dying. You swallow a lot of water, too. But I was so relieved when I found out what was wrong with me.

The canister I'd tucked into my belt before I made my one man abortive blitzkrieg on the *Ayacucho City*'s engineering staff had gradually slipped down inside the front of my trousers until it was trapped firmly where a tailor measures your leg length. Very kinky stuff. It was also bloody uncomfortable. I even had to kick my pants off before I could recover it but I didn't think it would matter all that much, the local residents of this patch were much more likely to find me edible than sexy. It made it easier to swim anyway.

I let go of the cylinder and it shot up to the surface like a cork. Swimming on a few yards I reflected on the odd things that people collect under stress, then I trod water again and looked back at the canister as it bobbed in my wake, a little yellow sliver in the moonlight.

Then I paddled back and, clutching it, opened the lid. The little green neon winked up at me in a comforting sort of way when I depressed the micro-switch, so I shrugged resignedly. For what it was worth I was now sailing in company with a green eyed tube that went by the name of FAT CAN.

The Equipment Research Branch of the Ministry of Defence had a much more inflated and sophisticated title for it – the Floatable Automatic Transmitting Canister Mk. III, but FAT CAN was rather more appropriate, and about as much bloody use.

Oh, admittedly I had a method of signalling my presence now. FAT CAN emitted a succession of sonic waves which could be traced to source in order to recover the cylinder itself – as with the grain samples I ditched off Gib. There were, in fact, only two snags – it required a vessel equipped with a HOT FAT CAN to find it, and only within a twenty-five mile range at that.

HOT FAT CAN . . . ? I didn't believe it either until the M.O.D. man assured me, without even the faintest trace of a smile, that the search ship was equipped with a Homing Oscillating Tracker.

Actually, once you'd stopped laughing, it was quite a clever device in that the recovery vessel operator – HOT FAT OP? – just read off the target's bearing and distance from a screen in front of him and the point of convergence was accurate to within two feet. In fact there was a vicious, slanderous story current in B.M.S.N.C. circles about the thing being so precise that, during its initial sea trials, the Naval minesweeper acting as recovery ship actually struck, and halved, the research craft within fifteen inches of the scientist holding FAT CAN.

But it still left me floating in the drink and bleeping like a lost sheep without the remotest hope of a shepherd finding me. The chances of any kind of ship being in my immediate area were slender enough, and completely non-existent for a ship equipped with a HOT FAT OP.

Apart from being a seaman I was also a highly trained specialist who could calculate the chances to within a degree. And I knew.

*

Which was why, when I glanced over my submerged shoulder an hour later, I was a little surprised to see a ship as big as a bloody mountain aiming straight for my head at twenty knots.

And I'd already seen her before. Very recently.

My already overstrung nervous system just dis-integrated. I can't remember anything about the next eternity of minutes except for the horror of splashing frantically away, fighting in terrified anticipation for the blessed safety of the black, cold sea out of range of her searchlight . . .

. . . and the lifeboat which smacked into the water from her port falls before she had even lost steerage way.

*

I was still fighting like a maniac when a pair of arms reached out for me like a great crab from the night, and plucked me into the bottomboards of the boat.

And I looked up into the shadowed face of Bosun

Clegg of *British Commander* just as the man at the tiller stood up threateningly.

Then McReadie's voice said irritably, 'If he doesn't stop bloody charging about, Bosun, sit on the silly bastard before he puts the lot of us in the bloody oggin!'

*

'Christ no, we weren't particularly looking for you,' McReadie said cheerfully. 'No. We've been keeping tabs on the Liberian since Gib – shadowing her on radar – but we were bound for Haifa anyway remember? With bulldozers and grub for the homeless. Or has our earthquake expert forgotten about the earthquake since he went for his pleasure cruise at the Company's expense?'

I lay there glowering at the deckhead of my own cabin, and felt the pain from my injured shoulder, and the sickness in my saline-saturated guts, and the frizzled, burnt flush of my skin – and waited for him to tell me I looked a lot better for it.

'Thanks! It was all a bundle of fun. Good food, lots to do . . . I mean, I only jumped over the fuggin' wall 'cause I was scared of getting soft in all that luxury . . .' I levered myself up on the arm that hadn't been hit by a ship's propeller and went dizzy, '. . . and anyway, why's J.C. made you come to sea with the real sailors, Commander? If this is just an ordinary humanitarian voyage?'

McReadie looked patronising. 'Did I say that?

187

Don't you appreciate the planning that went into scheduling us to slip in on the Liberian's tail while making the rest of the world think it was just co-incidence?'

'And it was just coincidence that you found me? Like running over a bottle of Coke in the Sahara Desert?' I desperately needed to feel wanted. Sought after.

All I got was an indifferent shrug. 'Thank Dave Ball for that, Cable. He kept the H.O.T. gear operating in case you tried to use the spare container to get another message to us. Personally I thought you were down among the dead men along with the rest of the *Ayacucho City*'s original crowd.'

I stared at him. 'How did you find out about that?'

'I told you we were tracking on radar. You stopped twice, the first time for about an hour and a half, the second for about six. We hove to and waited twenty miles astern. . . . There was a lot of wreckage the first time. What was it? That fishing boat?'

'Time bomb. The bastards! How'dyou find out it was a fisherman, though? That wreckage couldn't have been big enough to re-construct a bath tub model?'

'Med Section Intelligence have an agent in Sicily. He submitted a routine report saying an M.F.V. had been stolen from Syracuse harbour. Only reason it reached me was because we were particularly interested in this area. Then – if you're as clever as I am – two and two make four.'

The pains clawed up the side of my head again as I

188

jerked my chin aggressively, 'If you're so bloody sharp maybe you can tell me why we stopped for six hours the next day, too?'

McReadie stopped drinking my Board of Trade lime juice long enough to look surprised. 'Christ, don't you know yourself?'

That did it.

'Yes, I fuggin' do!' I yelled, 'It's just that I'm a bit bloody chokka with bein' bashed, drowned, melted down into a blob of grease an' tapped on the head by half the fuggin' shipping in the fuggin' Med . . .'

He smiled re-assuringly and patted my shoulder – the injured one. 'All right, they were contaminating the cargo, yes? We had a dry run on the way out with our own hatches, it takes just on six hours. They're very smart operators, Hosni's crowd.'

I flopped back and stared at him incredulously. '*Hosni's* crow. . . . You mean you knew? You bloody *knew*?'

McReadie shrugged. 'More or less. But we had to have more to go on than pure theory. You did happen to . . . ah . . . mention you weren't completely convinced yourself. Before you left for Halifax. Anyway, that Victor signal of yours was the clincher, we knew it could only be one kind of trouble. Actually J.C. figured that one out, mind you he's the sort of clever sod who does *The Times* crossword and that. I must say I thought it was a bit obscure, personally.'

I ignored the sour grapes. I wanted to find out what he could tell me about the calculating Hosni. Who was behind him? What motives made him tick? But there was another point I couldn't quite fathom.

'How did you know the Greeks had been given the deep six aboard the fishing boat? Or was that just theory, too?'

He pulled a face. 'We've got five and a half corpses stowed in the Chief Steward's cold stores ... five and three quarters, if you count another bucketful of bits. Hosni should have done it the messy way – shot the poor bastards at close range, then ditched them with a firebar for boots. How many were there anyway?'

I bit my lip. 'Over forty! Plus the Sparks and another quartermaster killed by the girl.'

'Girl? The Jordanian? Fathi al whatsit?'

'Mmmmm! But we guessed wrong there. She wasn't aboard to carry Anthrax-B, that must have been brought by the main group. The dolly was just there to make bloody sure no messages went out from the Liberian while she was being boarded ... and she did a very pro job of it! Oh, and the master – Argenti – he can be added to Hosni's score.'

McReadie didn't say anything for a few moments while I just lay back in my bunk thinking about poor old Argenti, and the nice little Greek radio op with the pyjama suit and the backless head. And how lovely it was to still be alive. Even with McReadie for company.

The glass in the rack over my bunk began to rattle persistently and I gradually became aware of the vibrations in the hull below me. We were obviously steaming hard, a lot faster than our normal cruising speed. But why ...? The *Ayacucho City* couldn't be doing more than seventeen knots while *Commander* was designed for a discreet twenty-four when no one was watching. If we kept going like this we'd be abeam of Hosni's ship within another two hours.

I stared curiously at McReadie who blinked back enigmatically. He glanced at the glass, too, then nodded. 'That's right, Mister. We're making emergency revolutions. Should be up with the Liberian at zero six two five.'

'And ...?'

'At zero six two six,' he murmured softly, '... we sink her.'

*

My watch said 4.55 a.m. Ninety minutes to go.

And I said, 'Bugger it!' then collapsed as far as my knees beside the bunk. McReadie bent down and helped me to a sitting position with a big grin on his face.

'Why do you tough bucko mates always think you're so indispensable?' he said unsympathetically. 'Especially when you've got me standing in for you.'

'That's what worries me,' I muttered viciously. 'Apart from which I'd rather be on deck in the fresh air when the action starts. Swimming's difficult enough without having the bloody ship round your neck.'

He shrugged. 'You make it sound like we're going to attack the *Bismarck*. She's only a cargo boat.'

A Plague of Sailors

I struggled to get my injured arm into my shirt. 'The best laid plans, etcetera. . . . You were going to brief me on Hosni, remember?'

He nodded and handed me a lighted Capstan. I think he enjoyed watching me sweat though, because he didn't lift a finger to help otherwise.

'Some of the background you already know.' He blew a smoke ring and poked at it with his finger. 'Born 1935. Egypt, some place called Qal'at al Akhdar. Not much known about his early life until he turned up in the Egyptian contingent to Dartmouth Naval College, class of '51 . . .'

I raised an eyebrow. That accounted for the polished presentation of the phoney H.M.S. *Diomede.*

'. . . Brilliant student – made some of our own embryo Nelsons look a bit sick – then went back home in time to see Farouk getting the chop from his own bloody kid, Ahmed Fuad.'

'And Hosni got the boot, too? In the *coup d'état?*'

'No. He was classified at that time as "Non-political". That meant he'd kept his nose clean and his mouth shut so far as Farouk's dolly birds were concerned. Anyway, he hung on in a junior lieutenant's berth on some ex-R.N., ex-Indian Navy, ex-First World War minesweeper, mostly swinging round a buoy in Port Said, until Neguib's military council kicked little King Fuad up the arse as well and took over the country.'

'Like musical bloody chairs,' I muttered, 'Then . . . ?'

'. . . Then he did finish up in some wog jail. Had a bad time as far as we know. But a comparatively unknown army officer called Lieutenant Colonel Gamal Abdel Nasser came along and it was time for all change hats at the Palace again. Hosni was released in January '55.'

'Back into the Navy?'

'Not to our knowledge, no. It seems he picked up some very extreme views while he was inside. Mostly anti-Zionist, but personally I think Nasser didn't dare take a chance on him biting the hand that released him. Anyway, for the past fifteen years or so he's been drifting from one berth to another in what's laughingly known as the United Arab Republic Mercantile Marine. And thinking, Cable boy. Thinking all the time. . . .'

I frowned. 'But he's working for Nasser's successor? This Anthrax-B project, it's a highly organised military operation. Unless you mean he's on Hussein's payroll now, or Syria's. There's a hell of a mixed crowd of Middle Eastern nationals working for him, like the girl being Jordanian and one jet black character in the deck gang who could even have been Sudanese. So who's behind him? Which country?'

McReadie popped another smoke ring and examined it closely.

'No one's backing Hosni,' he murmured. 'He's strictly a one man band.'

I stared at him. 'He's what . . . ? Oh look, Commander. Private armies are strictly for the story books.

Unless it's maybe in some African jungle backwater where time stopped moving fifty years ago.'

'You ever heard of Al Fatah?'

'The terrorists? Of course, but . . .'

'And the Popular Front for the Liberation of Palestine? Or the P.L.O., the Palestine Liberation Organisation?'

I nodded and McReadie spread his hands. 'So what d'you think they are if they're not private armies? And you said "Terrorists". Wouldn't that depend on whether you're a Jew or an Arab?'

I buttoned my shirt slowly. 'And Hosni's a member of one of those? Not a Sadat man at all?'

He shook his head. 'Hosni's only got one allegiance, Cable – hatred of the Israelis. Same old formula as the rest of the guerrilla organisations – Palestine for the Palestinians, Marxist-oriented resentment of Zionism, feudalism, imperialism and reactionary forces – but, and it's a big "But", Kamal Abul Hosni is a veritable eagle among the hawks . . . and he scares the hell out of the Arab League top brass.'

'Because of Israeli retaliation for what he might do?'

'Exactly. Which is why he has to depend on hand-outs and surreptitious gifts of non-standardised arms from secret sympathisers, while his commandos are a cosmopolitan crowd of drop-outs who got the push from the P.F.L.P. and Al Fatah 'cause they were too hot to handle.'

The time was 5.07 a.m.

I hauled on my white shorts and stood up gingerly.

This time I made it with only the faintest of tremors. 'I shouldn't have thought anyone was too bloody minded for the guerrillas. Aren't they engaged in a Holy Islamic crusade with the one intention of massacring every Jew in the Middle East? So where's the difference? Hosni's going to save them all that bother. In fact, the trouble then'll be to find enough *Arabs* left to walk back into Jerusalem.'

McReadie stubbed his cigarette out. 'The difference is that, even after the Jordanian civil war, the established mobs are still very dependent on the good will of people like Hussein and Sadat to provide them with bases. And so long as the Israelis don't push too hard in retaliation for the odd hijacking of an El Al Boeing or a grenade explosion in Dizengoff Street, then Damascus and Cairo will keep on pretending not to notice.'

'But get one bull in the Arabian china shop – like Hosni – and the balance of power gets upset, presumably? Al Fatah's got no home to go to while the political leaders get an Israeli rocket up the camel trail.'

McReadie grinned and nodded. 'Not only that. Al Fatah, for instance, runs on funds granted by the various governments. Mostly, in their case, from Libya, Kuwait and Saudi Arabia. . . . Same with the P.F.L.P. and the P.L.O. So if Hosni gets out of control and the clamp comes down on all the guerrillas because of him, then the first thing to happen is that the piggy bank's slammed shut.'

I dragged my canvas shoes on and looked at my battered Timex. Seventy-five minutes to sinking time. 'Apart from which, if the grain gets delivered but someone in Haifa twigs before distribution, the piggy banks are more likely to all go up in a puff of thermo-nuclear bloody smoke ... Hosni may be a patriot to some, Commander, but to me he's just a dangerous, twisted little bugger.'

McReadie turned at the door and smiled without a lot of humour. 'In another seventy-four minutes, Mister, Hosni's going to be just a plain dead little bugger!'

The glass in the rack seemed to rattle a little harder as I pulled my cabin door to behind me.

*

At the bottom of the bridge ladder I hesitated and looked up at McReadie. Something had been niggling me all the way up to the boat deck and I suddenly realised what it was – I hadn't seen a sign of any armament. And it seemed a bit odd to be going in to sink a ship in the good old furtive B.M.S.N.C. tradition without even knowing how we intended to.

Obviously they had something up their sleeve but, with my not being aboard when they sailed ex-U.K., I hadn't had time to catch up with today's selection of killing gear. Maybe it was a job for the *Ikara* missile already used on the too-inquisitive *Sovetskogo Soyuza* off Cape Wrath? Though that was more an anti-submarine weapon.

Or what about the mounting in number four 'tween decks for a twenty-one inch torpedo tube, behind the drop down hull section? Was it now occupied for the outward leg of voyage number sixteen?

Or even good old fashioned, unsophisticated surface gunfire by the 4.7's which could be concealed under the crated deck cargo forward? I hoped not. I hated those bastards aboard the *Ayacucho City* but I kept getting a vision of a beautiful girl with lovely legs shorn off below the knees by the white hot smash of a localised H.E. burst.

I mean, if it has to happen to her, then please God make it a bloody big, instantaneous bang. . . .

McReadie hesitated halfway up the bridge ladder when I asked him.

'Can't risk using anything that may leave evidence of intent, Cable. Too many curious people nosing round amongst the wreckage after. Asking awkward questions . . .' He looked down at me and smiled but, for the first time, I thought I detected a trace of tension in his voice.

'. . . that's why we're going to *ram* the Liberian. At twenty-four knots.'

*

It took me a long time to find my voice. All I managed to do was to climb the rest of the way to the bridge deck and struggle to look ruggedly casual while the Second Mate pumped my hand and seemed pleased as hell to see me again.

I forced a weak grin and mumbled something inadequate about 'Thanks, it was mostly due to you, Two Oh!', then hung around like a neurotic vulture at the after end of the bridge until I could grab McReadie and haul him to one side.

'Whadd'you mean – *ram* her, for Christ's sake?' I growled.

He shrugged and his face was an impassive white blob in the darkness. 'I've told you, Cable. This has got to be all strictly above suspicion. When the Israelis find that much vaunted Egyptian peace offering has somehow managed to get itself sunk on the way they're going to be . . . ah . . . cynical. To say the least. Unless accidental loss can be undisputably proved. Apart from which, as you know yourself, it's damned near impossible to sink a ship by remote control without leaving some tell-tale wreckage – maybe a lifebelt with a shell fragment in it, or a hatch board with amatol or cordite burns.'

I shook my head, feeling the old familiar sickness in my belly. 'Cut her in half and you'll need a fuggin' diversion sign round the gear she'll spew out when she goes!'

'So . . . ? The more the merrier, Mister. Obviously a tragic accident. Another collision at sea and let's all pretend to think about changing the International Regulations for rule of the road . . . but it's been established as an *accident*! And we steam into Haifa down by the head and with a smashed bow and sad expression to prove it.'

'At twenty-four bloody knots,' I muttered, 'we'll be steaming straight to the bottom as well, with a contertina'd hull and a dead expression instead. Christ, but I wish you'd left me in the water.'

McReadie shrugged indifferently again. 'So I promise not to shout "Man overboard" if you want to be discreetly sneaky.'

I ignored it. It wasn't funny and anyway right then even Charlie Chaplin would have seemed a funereal figure. Another thought struck me. 'Hasn't it occurred to you that there are nearly twenty very tough boys aboard Hosni's boat? Which means that – wherever we hit her – there must still be a lot of survivors, and all ready to blow the gaff on both the Anthrax *and* us when they're picked up. Because they're fanatics, McReadie. They won't keep their hatred quiet. And you've already said it – even the suspicion of what was planned could set the whole bloody world on fire.'

A click behind me made me half turn and I blinked. Out on the wing of the bridge dim figures moved smoothly as they lifted a heavy object into its mounting on the sanded teak rail. The ship rolled slowly and the first wash of dawn glinted softly on metal. I didn't need to look any longer, I'd seen one before.

A general purpose machine gun.

I swung back to see McReadie watching me closely. It also suddenly registered why he wasn't worrying about what the *Ayacucho City* survivors would say – because there just weren't going to *be* any.

But then, I was working for a firm who played in the

same league as Hosni. Except that we'd had a lot more practice. The only trouble was that I was too sick to face it any more, sick of all the tension, and the killing, and the getting myself into the position where, after an action, I had to go below and stare at my face in the mirror and ask if murder and patriotism weren't getting a little confused.

I said, 'No, McReadie! This time we've got to. . . .'

His face came within a few inches of mine and I suddenly stopped saying anything at all, shocked by the depth of feeling behind his deceptively casual exterior.

'You want to be a fuggin' humanitarian, Cable, you join the Salvation Army. But me, I'm thinking about the little kids at home with the melted eyeballs from an H-bomb flash, not the ethics, or even the deeper implications . . .'

I was aware of his fingers digging brutally into my aching shoulder but I didn't move away. I just bit my lip as his voice went very low, '. . . but stay off my back, Mister Mate! Stay off it or by Christ you *will* be down there in the bloody water again.'

He let me go but he hadn't quite finished. 'But you'll be face down, Cable. With a great big hole in your skull. And there isn't one man in B.M.S.N.C. who'd lift a finger to stop me, because they're fanatics too, Cable. And dedication doesn't leave room for the weak or the tired, or the bloody good chap.'

And I didn't think even Kamal Abul Hosni could have put his motives in a better way. Except that he would have been thinking about little Palestinian Arab kids, instead of British ones.

*

The *Ayacucho City* looked bigger than ever as we surged up astern of her in the early morning light. I stood nervously in the concealment of the wheelhouse – out of view of any prying binoculars – and gazed apprehensively over the helmsman's shoulder as the target ship just growed and growed, while the fuzzed white rectangles of her superstructure crystallised into clear-cut doors and portholes. And people.

The cool sweat from my eyebrows clung to the foam rubber eyepieces of the Barr and Stroud 10×50's as I raised them and vectored along her starboard alleyways towards her bridge. Two figures were leaning casually over the rails outside her engine room entrance on the centrecastle deck. One was dressed in white overalls and I wondered spitefully if he was the hot-shot submachine-gun operator who'd provided a nine millimetre orchestration to my tattooed tread tango last night. It struck me then that, if we had to make the hit, the spot where Machine gun Kelly stood was as good as any for starters.

A brief flash of colour from the prom deck. Raise the glasses fractionally – yes, there she was! Fathi al-Rana'i, Jordanian dolly girl extraordinary, of the lovely legs, sad eyes and positively devastating technique with Greek sailormen in pyjamas. A flutter of white – she was waving gaily at us just like any other ship's passenger would do in the lonely vastness of the ocean. Yes dear, we'll be dropping in any time now. . . .

Up again to Funnel House and the acrid taste of exhaust fumes biting in my throat, then forward to the Liberian's bridge. And Hosni.

I touched the knurled wheel with the ball of my middle finger and the dark, handsome figure leapt into sharp focus . . . Christ, but he has big round eyes . . . No, wait! Just gazing astern at us through his own binoculars, anxiously inspecting *British Commander* for the least signs of any suspicious activity. But he would never guess why we were coming up so close to his own wake. That he was looking at a ten thousand ton bullet aimed straight at him. . . . Another figure moved out to the wing of the bridge beside him and I caught the sparkle of a second pair of glasses giving us the third degree as I moved guiltily back into the shade of our chartroom door.

Though I knew they couldn't really have cause for doubt until it was too late, because we'd done all this before and we were very good at it. The old Lion often practised in sheep's clothing . . . or did that make us wolves? Like the buccaneers of old, or the rapacious U-boats of a quarter of a century ago. . . .

Then the Old Man and McReadie broke up their huddle out on the port wing beside the canvas camouflaged shape of the machine gun, and Second Mate Ball flicked the stub of his last cigarette away before he took up his post at the engine room telegraphs beside ex-Chief Petty Officer Bryant on the wheel.

And Chief Officer Brevet Cable checked for the twentieth time that his orange and blue life jacket lay nice and handy on the chart room settee behind him.

While Captain Caird stepped over the coaming into the wheelhouse and, picking up the engine room phone, said, 'Chief? I estimate another six minutes to impact. Get everyone up on deck apart from yourself and the Second. And . . . good luck, Wilf!'

I never realised a ship could look so big and solid as the *Ayacucho City* did right then.

And unsinkable.

*

Out attack plan was simple – and timed to the last second in little pencilled notations on the plot of convergence which was laid out on the ledge at the forr'ad end of the wheelhouse. I moved up beside Ball and glanced at the neatly drawn courses charted in red and blue – blue for the target ship, red for *Commander*. Blood red.

Five minutes to impact.

Biting my lip I compared the red arrow marked *I minus 5* with our actual position in relation to the Liberian. We should now be running parallel with her and some three cables astern, with a half mile gap between the ships . . . yes, there she was, kicking up white water over on our port side, slightly on the bow. Still unsuspecting, presumably, even though we were a lot closer than most overtaking ships would be. But then, under the International regulations, she was the 'stand on' vessel and would be relying on our watch-keeper to stay clear.

A movement from McReadie out on the port wing and a glint of early morning sunlight from the instrument he held in his hands. A Stuart's Distance Meter, normally used for station keeping as a range finder on the next ship but now virtually relegated to the obsolete locker other than for Fleet reviews. And pre-planned collisions! He turned and gestured slightly to Caird . . . Close up!

'Come three degrees to port, Bryant.' The Old Man glanced at me and smiled fractionally through the strained creases around his mouth. 'All my life I've been worrying about collision at sea, Mister. It took Commander McReadie's fancy Navy ways to show me how bloody difficult it is to arrange one.'

I grinned half-heartedly back, knowing he was only being cynical. Collisions are easy to organise, even without trying, but it's not so damned easy to hit a seventeen knot ship in the right place and at just the right time . . . and so you can come astern out of the hole you've made and still float while the other poor bastards go down like an express train.

The Old Man had other worries too. Like how to hang on to his master's ticket after the inevitable court of inquiry had queried how in God's name it was possible for two ships on the same course to collide in brilliant sunlight on an empty ocean. Without even one survivor left to put the other vessel's point of view. . . .

Bryant sang out, 'Steady on 094, Sir!' and I glanced at the bulkhead clock.

Four minutes to Impact.

The Second Mate shifted nervously beside me, hands toying with the bright brass handles of the telegraph. I blinked as I heard him singing under his breath, 'We all live in a yellow submarine ... a yellow submari...'

'Shut up f'r Chrissake!' I muttered and he threw me a hurt look. I didn't care though. Submarines were the one thing I wanted to keep at the back of my mind right now.

Three minutes thirty seconds.

The red line on the plot broke away from its parallel track here, beginning to converge on the straight blue course of the *Ayacucho City*. A blob of sweat trickled down my nose and splashed on the white paper just at the critical point – where the red arrows curved round almost at right angles and merged into the blue ... and there was only snowy, pristine paper from that point on ... Jeeeeze but I'd be sick if I only had the guts, in front of all these bloody impassive faces. ...

'Port ten the wheel.' The Old Man's voice was tight.

'Port ten of wheel, Sir ... Wheel ten degrees to port, Sir.'

The horizon started slipping over to the right and a flutter of spray climbed our port bow to straddle hissingly across our number one hatch cover. The sea was getting up, slapping angrily at our plates as we broadsided into it. Was it a warning? But surely not even Hosni could have God – or was it Mohammed? – on his side? Not with what he intended to do to the world. My legs felt shaky and I prodded irritably at the pencil which was starting to rattle under the vibration of our pounding engines.

McReadie called urgently from the wing, 'Aldis!'

I grabbed the lamp from the locker and went out into the bright sunlight, half crouching below the level of the innocuously armour plated bridge front. Everything had to look casual from the *Ayacucho City*, only the one expected watchkeeper on our bridge, a specially arranged work party painting disinterestedly on the – we assumed – safety of our poop. The bloody Aldis cable got itself entangled under the wheelhouse door and I jerked savagely to free it.

McReadie murmured, 'Butterfingers,' and grinned sardonically but I just showed him a tightly stretched backside as I scrambled back into the concealment of the wheelhouse, hating him every inch of the way.

Three minutes.

'Ten more to port.'

'Ten more to port . . . twenty of port wheel on, Sir.'

Oh Christ!

The Old Man lowered his binoculars. 'They're starting to get worried, McReadie.'

I dragged my own glasses up to my eyes – *They* were, for Harry's sake . . . Hosni's ship looked as big as a cathedral when she slammed into focus. Almost abeam of us now and maybe three cables away, still closing fast. The starboard wing of her bridge looked so near I could have reached out and punched Hosni right on his dark, aquiline nose. . . . I could almost see the look of consternation and indecision on his features.

But then, the officers of the *Titanic* couldn't have looked exactly complacent either, when a hundred thousand tons of ice suddenly reared out of the sea and fell on them.

A fleeting glance at the plot. We still had to draw slightly further ahead of them than we were at present to allow for the loss of forward momentum when we turned hard in. Into her engine space just abaft the high bridge. The big red cross where the lines ceased grew all fuzzy and started to look like a question mark so I gripped the binoculars viciously to stop my hands trembling.

Get me out of this, God, and I'll . . . I'll even keep bloody chickens on that bloody overdue farm. Beady eyes an' all, so help me!

'We all live honna yellow submarine . . . ha *yeller* submarine . . . ha yeller submareeeeeen.'

Fuggin' second mates. Never could keep their mouths shut. . . .

Two minutes. Where the hell *did* I leave that lifejacket?

The Old Man's voice cut across the silence. 'Aldis, McReadie. Lot of commotion on her bridge now, they're going to alter away from us.'

I saw the stubby cylinder of the Aldis swing up to McReadie's shoulder and smiled bitterly. We were using every dirty trick in the book to play for more time, to distract their attention over on the Liberian's bridge while we crept up in position for the kill.

His finger went round the trigger and the shutter started to clack, loud in the tension filled air . . . Long, short, short, long . . . X . . . X . . . X . . . Cheeky bastard, McReadie! . . . Single letter code for 'Stop carrying out your intentions and watch for my signals'.

But the next signal Hosni would get would be the big vee sign of our bows giving him a sailor's farewell before they smeared him right across his bridge deck and pushed the whole bloody lot over into the sea.

It seemed to work, though. I watched as Hosni half turned towards the wheelhouse then hesitated while he tried to digest the import of our crazy instruction. It was a natural reaction for any seaman, and Hosni was a seaman without doubt.

Suddenly a movement, in the periphery of my binocular-limited vision. Someone running forward along their boat deck? What the . . . ? He's carrying something over his shoulder . . . a pole? A . . . ah, what the hell! The man vanished behind the white blanket of number one starboard lifeboat and I forgot all about him.

One minute to death time, and we seemed exactly on course.

I moved back towards the chart room door, gripping the frame tightly in anticipation and feeling the pain from my injured arm bite dully into my shoulder. It didn't matter anymore, though. I was about to pay Hosni back for that underwater punch with about ten thousand foot-tons interest.

A final sight of McReadie dropping the Aldis and running for the shelter of the after end of the bridge, then I raised my eyes fractionally to see we were now slightly ahead of the *Ayacucho City* with our midships section in line with her flared bows.

And the Old Man's voice bellowing 'Hard a port!' while the wheel blurred under Bryant's hands as our masts careered crazily across the line of the sea, canting twenty degrees to starboard under the pull of the turn.

I only realised things were going wrong when the lurching swing flung me drunkenly against the chart room door, and the *Ayacucho City* blotted out the sunlight right across our wheelhouse windows while her great siren started to shriek a warning. . . .

I saw Second Mate Ball clinging to the shiny column of the telegraphs while his lips opened wide to scream, 'Holy Mother, but we've left it too fuggin' late . . . We've overshot! Goin' right across her bloody bows . . . !'

And the Old Man started to roar 'Half astern, port engi . . . !' but never managed to complete the sentence that would have pulled our bow round faster and saved us.

Because his head, still with a very self-reproachful expression fixed on the sunburned features, abruptly flew off his shoulders and bounced twice along the sanded teak rail before it finally ricocheted into the sea.

Along with most of ex-Chief Petty Officer Bryant's upper torso, Second Mate Ball's forearms – still clinging dutifully to the brass telegraph handles – and my bloody hat.

My very best one.

Chapter Six

When you're unconscious and down on your hands and knees you get a completely different impression of things. Which was why, for a few moments, I didn't really think there was anything particularly odd about the Captain's standing there without a head, beside half a helmsman and an armless, rather surprised looking, second mate.

Then the Old Man and the late Alf Bryant R.N., retd. sort of keeled inwards towards one another and slopped to the deck like an unfinished jigsaw puzzle, while Dave Ball quarter-turned, gazed blankly at me, and waggled his stumps of arms a bit vaguely.

And McReadie slammed through the wheelhouse doors without his usual debonair aplomb, and yelled, 'They had a fuggin' gun, Cable! You never said they had a fug . . . !'

But the Second Mate started to scream then and I never did hear the end of McReadie's complaint because I was too busy trying to find my best cap amongst the glass shards and splintered fittings which littered the compo deck, and all the time getting more and more irritated with the droplets of blood that kept running down the side of my face and spraying over the backs of my hands . . .

... until McReadie grabbed me by the shoulders, slapping me back into the horrors of the present, and I surged partially out of my state of shock just in time to see Dave Ball – still screaming dreadfully – run blindly in a complete circle out on the starboard wing before he crashed head over heels down the near vertical ladder to the boat deck.

McReadie shouted urgently, 'Get the hell out've here, Cable! Starboard door ... She's going to hit us right under the bloody bridge!'

But I knew *that* much already. Because I could see Hosni's death ship over McReadie's shoulder.

And she was only twenty feet away.

*

Then horror piled upon horror and everything seemed to happen all at once, but in a curiously slow-motion way that etched every impression deep in my memory.

I remember a bird's eye view of the *Ayacucho City*'s foc'slehead sliding in at right angles below us, still with a tall, dark-skinned man staring up in paralysed terror from abaft the windlass, the look of death in his eyes and a paintbrush in his hand.

I thought detachedly, 'What a funny thing for a pirate to be doing, painting ship.' Then I noticed the scarred ventilators and rails and remembered the shot from the counterfeit H.M.S. *Diomede* so long ago, and realised that Hosni could hardly take a battle scarred freighter into Haifa without exciting a lot of unwelcome curiosity.

In another three seconds he was going to need a helluva lot more than a pot of white paint and a two inch brush. *And* he was going to have to find a new painter, too.

Then the Liberian's forepart was blanked out by the wing of our bridge and all I could see was the crucifix of her foremasthead quartering a great, blaring, familiar yellow funnel while the row of her wheelhouse windows gleamed like square, ebony teeth in a corpse-white face ... and a small figure which must have been Hosni staring, transfixed, over the canvas dodgers at her bridge front ...

... gradually I felt McReadie tugging frantically at my shoulder, but I knew we were both dead already so I couldn't help grinning stupidly through the red haze of blood as I heard myself giggling, 'Christ, but J.C.'s goin' to be a bit annoyed with us, chum. ...'

The *Ayacucho City* carved into us, ripping a vertical gash that obliterated our vegetable room, our evaporator room, our switchboard flat and our Chief and Second Engineers.

We'd started to sink before McReadie could drag me even half-way to the starboard wheelhouse door.

*

Ships involved in a collision don't just stop dead, like that. They keep on going, on and on, for a very long time. Like the *Ayacucho City* was doing as she tried to roll right on over us.

We started to fall over to starboard while I clung

dazedly to the shorn-off column of the telemotor and just stared uncomprehendingly at the polished brass inclinometer on the after bulkhead as it recorded our amount of list . . . Twenty-five degrees . . . thirty . . . thirty bloody five she must be lying with her centre-castle decks awaaaaash! . . . forty? . . . Forty-fiiiiive? . . . Forty-six, I was staring downwards over the flat plane of the wing, right into the sea itself . . . forty-seve . . . !

The rest of Captain Caird and C.P.O. Bryant slid erratically past me down the chute and I started to be sick at an angle of fifty degrees from the vertical.

At fifty-two degrees I saw someone waving feebly to me from the floor . . . the floor? The Goddamned *water*. Then I remembered that most of *Commander*'s crewmen had been ordered to stay on deck, spread along the concealed starboard alleyways. Just in case. And now the 'in case' had happened and we'd have been as well issuing them with a millstone each to go around their necks because, by now, most of them would have difficulty in swimming seeing there was a whole fuggin' ship lying on top of them. . . .

At fifty-five degrees McReadie couldn't hold on to his particular little bit of ship any longer, and came roller-coasting down towards me. I let go of the telemotor thinking it didn't make much difference now anyway, and we avalanched in company to crash against the sidescreens of the wheelhouse.

I couldn't resist it. I twisted my head, stared wildly into McReadie's screwed-up eyes, and screamed

'Butterfingers, you bastard!' in a hysterical voice. Then McReadie put his arms around me and I started to cry with the fear of it all while the rending and tearing and shrieking went on and on and on. . . .

At sixty degrees we stopped capsizing. And everything was as silent as the breath of a dead man. Until, a million miles away, we heard the clang of a bridge telegraph.

As the *Ayacucho City* started to back out of the huge wound she'd slashed in our side.

And the sea started to thunder in.

*

When I was little I used to have one of those funny celluloid men with a big round bottom, the kind that won't lie down no matter how hard you push at them.

Commander had a big round bottom too. Which was why, when the Mediterranean started to collapse into her at the rate of several hundred tons a minute she acted – for a very short time – like my funny little man and fought to swing back to the vertical.

The trouble was that McReadie and I, up in her morgue of a wheelhouse, described a precisely similar arc to the little man's head – except that the circumference of our travel was at the dizzy end of an eighty foot radius.

And it knocks the hell out of your equilibrium.

I lay for a few moments trying to figure out how I could have been standing on the bulkhead one minute and be flat on my back on the deck the next. All

215

without moving one aching muscle. Then McReadie seemed to get really anxious to leave because he grabbed me by the front of my blood-stained shirt and literally dragged me to my feet.

When he slammed me across the face with the back of his hand, I only stopped getting mad when I realised the deck had started to slope again, but this time in a different direction. I did a funny, tripping stagger to the fore end of the bridge and stared blankly at where our foc'slehead should have been.

I saw the sea.

Jesus!

Then the *Ayacucho City* gave another great tug astern and I swung around to see she was still doggedly boring into our side, practically underneath where I stood, and that I couldn't see *her* foc'slehead either because it was enmeshed along with our vegetable room, switchboard flat, number six double bottom tanks and the huge space that had been our sparkling engine room.

At least Chief Elliot and the Second had company. In the shape of a tall dark corpse with a white paint-brush in its hand.

McReadie slapped me across the face a second time and I blinked at him with hurt eyes. The third slap finally brought me round and I started to realise I wasn't floating on the fringes of a maniac's nightmare — that this was actually happening, and that the grinding screech of tortured metal below me was signalling that *British Commander* had very few minutes left to live.

He forced a nervously sardonic grin. 'C'mon, Cable! Or aren't you so bloody keen to go over the wall now, hah?'

Then the whole bridge deck seemed to jump three feet in the air, and McReadie stopped grinning as we fell against each other and did an involuntary foxtrot downhill – this time to the port side.

I had one brief glimpse of the *Ayacucho City*'s length, with the white water pulsating forward along the red slash of her anti-fouling as her huge screws threshed convulsively astern . . . until my eyes focused on a familiar grey square which looked ridiculously like her number one hatch cover . . . but couldn't be because that meant. . . .

Then the whole world slammed sideways as she finally dragged herself clear of the belly wound in *Commander*, and I looked up to see our funnel and wheelhouse and monkey island and McReadie all toppling down on me at the same bloody time. . . .

I was glad of the blackness when the discarded Aldis disconcertingly leapt six feet in the air and bounced off the side of my head. I didn't want to have to drown while I was still aware of being alive.

*

Fug Vice-Admiral Sir James Cromer V.C. etc.

McReadie slapped me across the face again and I shook my floating head resentfully, not wanting to wake up in time for dying. Anyway, it wasn't a habit I wanted him to develop.

I snapped 'All right, all *right*, f'r Pete's sake!' then levered my gummed eyelids open just enough to feel mildly curious about how McReadie had managed to hit me when he was a good twenty feet away, sitting all hunched up with his head between his knees and not looking at all debonair or cynical.

The large Arab standing over me didn't look particularly debonair, either – just plain bloody mad.

I closed my eyes with a groan and hoped he would slap me again. It promised to be a lot less destructive than the Decteriov submachine gun barrel that ground in below my left ear.

*

But that was ridiculous! We didn't *have* any Arabs aboard *British Commander*. And even if we did they'd be jumping over the wall along with anyone else who didn't particularly want to go down with the ship.

So . . . ?

A staccato order from somewhere up in the sky above, then the Decteriov withdrew from my ear while I heard McReadie retching painfully in the middle distance.

Half a minute later I still couldn't quite place the Arab and I still hadn't solved the puzzle of the Heavenly voice, so I opened my eyes very, very cautiously for the second time.

And thought, 'What a funny thing. I've never seen a ship's bridge on another ship's foc'slehead before. . . .'

Then I sat up involuntarily, gazing round like a drooling idiot and completely ignoring the silent, menacing ring of gun-slung dark men around me, then stared out over the *Ayacucho City's* bulwarks – out past McReadie's hunched shoulders as he clung shakily for support – out to where what was left of *British Commander* formed a centrepiece to the half mile of sea between us.

I wasn't really surprised to find she looked sadly forlorn and emasculated without her bridge deck, because I knew I'd seen the surplus one balanced across the Liberian's forward end before. Which also accounted for McReadie and myself enjoying Kamal Abul Hosni's shipboard hospitality, in that we'd just completed the most elaborate and expensive ship to ship transfer in maritime history.

I bit my lip and guessed that the B.M.S.N.C. Lion must be burying his hoary old head in shame right now. Just like *Commander* was burying hers as she lay tiredly in the blue chop of the Mediterranean. Even from where we watched I could see her once sleek hull was now gashed and broken, with the forepart already well under and her entrails all fuzzed and vague behind the erupting foam of the encroaching sea.

Then she daintily lifted her stern a bit higher until the dull gleam of her frozen screws was joined to the sea by a silvery, twinkling cascade of water, but it stopped being pretty when her after mast slowly keeled forward and sliced into the snowy white block of her centrecastle, sweeping her funnel forwards and downwards, and compacting it into the cavity left by the amputated bridge perching so ridiculously beside me.

McReadie muttered sickly, 'She's going, Cable. God help them.'

Our Father which art in Heaven . . . stop crying you bloody fool, everybody's watching . . . and you can't remember the words anyway. But the sadness is there, and the memories . . . God, but she was a bloody lovely ship. . . .

The tiny bulldozers on her after deck rolled over the side like vagrant yellow marbles as her bulkheads collapsed, and the thunder of her going echoed in a roar of defiance – a Lion's roar. Then only the last bleeding finger of her Red Ensign projecting from the seething blister over her grave.

And even that was gone, until the fuel oil surfaced from her imploding double bottoms and the last memory I had of her was a shiny round, spreading abcess on the water, with a lot of floating, distorted shapes drifting sluggishly with nowhere to go, and not one of them moving. Not one. . . .

It seemed a very long way to the bridge, on the end of a gun.

And Hosni's frustrated anger.

*

McReadie only managed to get half-way up the ladder from the promenade deck, then he fell over backwards and went clattering all the way down again. I couldn't help feeling a bit superior after reflecting on the pounding I'd taken over the past two days, so I muttered 'Cissie!' under my breath, then felt a twinge of guilt because the gash on his head was bleeding a lot worse than mine.

I was quite glad of the diversion though. It gave me time to sag against the cutwater of number one starboard boat and make an assessment of the damage done to the *Ayacucho City* while Hosni's commandos kicked the Commander around a little before aiming him back at the ladder again.

The first thing I noticed was that there wasn't any vibration from the engines, which meant presumably that Hosni had stopped them on dragging clear of *Commander* until he could sum up the situation and receive his damage control reports. We lay as dead in the water as those black little humps half a mile away.

There were a lot of curious little shapes scattered around the Liberian's number one hatch as well and it took me a few moments to realise that they were potatoes and carrots and onions, which seemed pretty odd things to leave lying around on a ship's deck until I remembered our eviscerated vegetable room.

There was something else scattered around too, but the only bit I could recognise was a white paintbrush.

I ran my eye further forward, past the chipped barrels of the cargo winches towards the break of the foc'slehead. But there wasn't one. just that damned great slab of *Commander*'s bridge deck balanced precariously over the concertina'd, compacted stub of what had been a beautifully flared bow only a few minutes ago.

I also felt the angle of the deck under my feet as it sloped ever so slightly towards the sea. 'She's down by the head,' I thought which – considering the amount of water that must have been in her shattered number one lower hold – didn't need a naval architect to work out.

Her hold? Then her cargo must be . . . Christ! The anthrax!

The nausea swept over me along with the realisation. With all the terror and desperate struggle for life of the preceding minutes I'd completely forgotten *why* we'd just sacrificed seventy of *Commander*'s crewmen. The whole reason for their dying.

And now they were already gone, while McReadie and I stumbled towards our own private little appointment with death on the end of a terrorist's submachine-gun barrel – yet five of the six holds beneath me still contained enough contaminated grain to kill a large slice of the human race twelve hours after eating lunch.

And maybe the rest of the world in a surge of thermo-nuclear instant peevishness.

McReadie blundered into me looking like a man who'd been badly beaten up by an Arab. I started to move ingratiatingly towards the bridge ladder, then reluctantly returned and – slinging McReadie's limp arm around my neck – half dragged him along with me, leaving a twin-track of blood for the thuggery to follow.

I'd forgotten all about Anthrax-B again.

It's funny how the rest of the world's problems can recede when you're in a bloody awful mess yourself.

If you're scared sick. Like me.

*

Hosni didn't say anything for a few moments. But then again, he didn't shoot us quite as quickly as he did the late Captain Constantine Argenti either. I felt a bit like a condemned man who'd been sent to Coventry instead.

I also felt very tired and very ill. I hoped McReadie wouldn't mind too much when I let him go and he slumped to the deck like a garden worm which had unexpectedly been stood on end. I wanted very much to join him but a silly desire to hear the old Lion get up and growl again, just a little, made me cling to the vertical as long as possible.

When Hosni finally spoke it was in the same impeccably English voice I'd heard once before – over a loud hailer in the middle of the night. Except that, this time, there was an indefinable edge of barely controlled anger to it.

'Your name, please?'

I tried to glower. 'Smith. Chief Officer. And why the bloody hell did you sink my ship?'

He didn't look surprised, he just nodded fractionally and the man behind kicked me in the kidneys. When they'd dragged me back to my feet with the cold sweat pouring down the side of my face and splashing his nice

deck with saline-diluted bloodstains, he spoke again.
Quite pleasantly.

'Your name, please . . . Chief Officer?'

I grated, 'Smith for Christ's sake. Albert Smith. . . .'

Then the girl Fathi appeared at the top of the ladder,
and looked very surprised and said 'Mister *Cable* . . .',
and it was Hands, Boots and Bumpsy Daisy a second
time.

I think it was the irritating pitch of my scream more
than the humanitarian considerations which made
Hosni stop them before they actually kicked my spine
up through the top of my skull. Then I was assisted
back up for Round Three without even a bottle of
water and a wet sponge.

'Your *name*. And that of the other man?'

I noticed he dropped the 'please' that time, but
I didn't make an issue of it. 'Cable. Brevet bloody
Cable . . . First Officer Brevet bloody Cable of the
British Mutual Steam Navigation . . . bloody . . . Com-
pany.'

'And the other man?'

I shrugged painfully. 'He's nobody. Just one of the
crowd. Second assistant lamptrimmer's mate, third
class. . . . He's no use to you.'

I hoped the second assistant lamptrimmer's mate,
third class, couldn't hear me. Describing your employer's operations superintendent like that could get a
bloke fired. But, then again, under the present
circumstances. . . .

The girl frowned at me with those big dark eyes and

224

drew Hosni aside, talking to him in low tones. When he turned round he gazed at me with a funny mixture of disbelief, curiosity and . . . admiration?

'Cable . . . ? Do you really mean the Cable who recently created havoc in my engine space then . . . ah . . . left us so abruptly? And rather later than we had originally surmised.'

There wasn't a lot of point in being secretive and modest. It couldn't serve any really useful purpose because we were dead anyway, and the anthrax would still get to Haifa, and they'd just keep on kicking me until I said 'yes.'

So I said, 'Yes.'

He smiled then, just a little, and raised an eyebrow in the same negligently casual way that McReadie used to. When he *had* eyebrows to raise. I wondered inconsequentially if they maybe taught them all to do that at Dartmouth Naval College.

I risked adding, 'But to me, Hosni, it's not "your engine space". You only borrowed it, you bastard.'

He was bloody flameproof. But then, not only did he hold all the aces, he was clinging on to the rest of the pack as well. 'You know my name then. . . . And what you really mean is that I'm a pirate, don't you, Mister Cable? A pirate and a . . . cold blooded murderer?'

'You said it, not me,' I muttered, taken aback by his unexpected candour and feeling angrily resentful that I wouldn't even have the satisfaction of insulting him before I got the deep six.

'To the Spaniards, Sir Francis Drake was a pirate, Cable. But, to you Englishmen, he was a patriot. . . .' He held up a hand as I started to mutter, '. . . No, please, I'm sorry but we don't have time to enter into an ethical debate for obvious reasons. I only submit a point of view.'

Which suited me perfectly because I couldn't help thinking of the role we played in B.M.S.N.C., and how the Reds would describe us if they only knew. And I couldn't find one argument to fight Hosni on because, by the same criterion, I was a pirate and a murderer too.

'More important – your ship, *British Commander*, Cable. She deliberately turned into me. Yet merchant ships just don't act like that . . . so what is so extraordinary about ships flying the B.M.S.N.C. house flag? You obviously had a reason, in fact a clear cut mandate, to attempt to sink me. . . .'

I grinned sickly through my fear, 'Get stuffed, Hosni. Shoot us, but don't be too bloody greedy for knowledge!'

Then I tensed my aching muscles, waiting for the slam in the kidneys from the rearguard, and the torment of agony that would follow. But I knew, without any heroics, that I could never tell them about J.C. and the ships with the *British* prefix because, if I did that, then all the reasons I had to die with a little bit of self-respect would have gone. And I badly needed a reason, at the very least.

Hosni said mildly, 'All right, Cable. Then perhaps

you would explain how much you know about my reasons for taking this ship the rest of the way to Haifa?'

I blinked in dazed relief when the anticipated blow didn't come. Then I shrugged. 'Enough.'

'Even about our cargo? But then, presumably you must in order to have been put aboard this ship in Halifax as a spy. You worry me a little, Cable. Who else knows . . . certainly not the Israelis, as yet.'

'You're being very careful with your words all of a sudden, Hosni? Why don't you say it . . . ? Say "I'm the Islamic *patriot* who's going to decompose the living bodies of every trusting little Jewish kiddy in the Middle East, just so's I can further the Great Arabian Revolution" . . . Go on, *say* it, Hosni. The key word is *anthrax*. It kills cows as well, and puppy dogs, and bloody camels and sheep and . . . and bloody *Arabs* too, Hosni . . . !'

He didn't nod this time but obviously the bloke behind me was a bit of an individualist because I went down just the same. And when I finally dragged myself up and peered at Hosni through tear-filled eyes he was talking animatedly to a newcomer on the bridge, a man in a stained white boiler suit with a coiled sounding line in his hand.

I stole a quick glance at the inert body of McReadie lying in a self-made pool of blood at my feet. He looked more or less dead and – while I started to feel cold and strangely sad at the realisation – I couldn't help being a little jealous of the peace he'd found as well.

But it felt very lonely. Without McReadie.

When Hosni turned back to me he was frowning thoughtfully. I caught sight of the girl watching me in concern, but only in the way a big sister would watch her brother when he'd scratched his knee very slightly. Then Hosni spoke again.

'We will continue our discussion later, Cable. You still have to tell me about your owner's rather ... ah ... extraordinary policies. Oh, and just how many more people are aware of the anthrax below. I'd like to know that, for when we arrive in Haifa. And you really will tell me, you know ...' He smiled slightly, almost apologetically, '... there is no more inventive an interrogator than ... a *bloody* Arab.'

'The whole civilised world knows about you, Hosni. You're flogging a dead horse, carrying on to the Holy Land.'

He shook his head and I knew I'd wasted my breath. 'I don't think so, Cable, I really don't think so. Or else you would have stopped me with a warship, quite openly. But then, I rather imagine your British Government would be loath to admit to their ... ah ... indiscretions. ...' He smiled again. 'No. Resign yourself to the fact that this ship will arrive in Haifa the day after tomorrow – late but still eagerly awaited – and by the day after, Palestine will become home once again for the Arab, while my freedom fighters will be recognised as the greatest ...'

I wished to God McReadie was with me. '... the greatest what, Hosni? The greatest scourge of humanity since the seven plagues of Egypt?'

He shrugged and turned away. 'Then perhaps, after such a series of cataclysms, it is my country's turn to become great again.'

I didn't laugh. They wouldn't have let me finish anyway.

McReadie's head bumped down every step as they dragged him to one of the late Greek officers' cabins. He didn't seem to mind, though. You usually don't – not when you're dead.

I heard bells when it was my turn to be kicked down the ladder. But they were only the engine room telegraphs ringing down for 'Half astern both'.

We started to shudder slowly round in a great semi-circle until our rudder pointed towards the rising sun, and we settled on a backwards course for the red cloud over Israel.

The bloody silly bridge across our bow followed like an obedient, batwinged spaniel.

*

The rest of that day passed in a haze of twilight delirium similar to a period which seemed a very long time ago, when I was aboard this very same ship but living in the top of a funnel.

I wasn't slowly asphyxiating this time though, I was just bleeding to death which was equally uncomfortable and very much messier. The succession of armed guards – who all lounged with their backs against the bulkhead and their feet up on the only bunk while McReadie and I sprawled on the deck – didn't seem to mind too much about the spreading crimson stains. But then, we'd already chopped the front off their ship and littered the rest of it with five hundred tons of scrap so they'd probably given up being house proud.

Every so often I kept coming round with a horrible, shivery start, to see a new, impassively watching face above a rag-tag and bobtail assortment of machine gun barrels, then I'd become aware of the racking shudder of the deck below me as the abused engines clawed us painfully slowly towards Haifa, and the yellow circle of the porthole-shaded sun spiralled in gentle, erratic whorls across the deck under the slow roll of the ship.

Once I tried to crawl to where McReadie lay un-moving, over to the corner where they'd thrown him. The click of a Sten safety catch discouraged my Good Samaritan approach and I flopped back thinking it didn't matter very much anyway because I wouldn't know the last rites for a dying man if I saw them on sale in a shop window. And if he was already dead, then he wouldn't need them.

Nice chap, McReadie. One of the very best. . . . And J.C.? Yes, he's a nice chap too. We were all jolly nice chaps, all of us. . . . And please God. If I say Hosni's a jolly nice chap as well, will you for pity's sake let me die before the uncivilised, camel riding, soulless bastard sets his bloody boys on me to find out the answers I haven't got the guts to refuse to give . . . not when they're digging my eyes out . . . and my . . .

. . . She's got nice legs though, Fathi al whatsit.

Bloody nice legs. Better than Hosni's, or J.C.'s. Or does J.C. *have* legs . . . ? Maybe he just moves around on castors . . . like a super robot. At least he's still got arms, though. Not like poor bloody drowned Second Mate Ball . . . 'cause you can't swim, not without arms. . . .

What was that thing about the admiral?

Fug 'im!

That's right.

*

They came to kill me just before it got too dark to see over the sights of a gun.

Then I remembered my appointment with the quiz-masters before the main event of Cable's evening started, and found I couldn't stop the nervous shudders which kept drumming my bound heels on the deck with embarrassing uncontrollability. I noticed dis-interestedly that I'd stopped bleeding at some point during the preceding timelessness of waiting – or maybe I'd just temporarily run out of plasma. Either way, I had a niggling suspicion I would be starting again very soon.

McReadie had stopped bleeding too, but I reflected sickly that, though we'd been lying here for nearly twelve hours, he hadn't moved. Not once. And that just wasn't possible for anyone with nerves and sinews and tendons still capable of suffering the pains of immobility.

Lucky, lucky bastard!

There were two of them in the little cabin, now. One – our current jailer – only seemed to be armed with the usual standard machine pistol and, on his own, I might have been tempted to make one last crazy, futile stab at escape. But even then – to where? Over the wall like the last time? And without even FAT CAN for company? And anyway, I'd already found that drowning was much the same as being shot. It just took a little longer.

It was the sight of the other bloke which finally put me off being a hero, the one who'd just come down to escort me to Hosni's little chat. He looked more like a high explosive Christmas tree than a maritime commando. I'd noticed that a lot of these freedom fighting guerrilla types had a penchant for covering themselves with all the weapons they could get their hands on, but this character was ridiculous.

He wasn't a soldier, he was a bloody munitions factory on legs.

First there were the criss-crossed bandoliers across his barrel chest, stencilled U.S. ARMY and stuffed with the bright shiny cones of nine millimetre short rounds. Then the inevitable S.M.G. – in his case a shiny new Che Guevara with a fold-over stock, *plus* a slung Mk. III Sten and finally, sagging in its web holster, an old and faithful Webley Scott .38.

He had a knife, too, though I didn't think he'd ever be reduced to actually needing it.

But what made me really decide on a strictly pacifist policy was the incredible assortment of mini-bombs he wore attached to the British Army surplus web belt round his waist. He positively clanked with the swing of Mills Grenades and Russian RG-42 anti-personnel canisters that looked just like a tin of beans without the label. I blinked involuntarily when I recognised even the antiquated shapes of the old 1914 German egg and oyster bombs while, hung in obvious pride of place right down his trouser buttons, was the *pièce de résistance* – a bloody great Red Army RPG-43 anti-tank hand grenade that could penetrate 2.95 inches of armour plating without trying.

And if *that* went off in the position it hung, then Abdul the Magnificent would definitely be wasting his time thinking about girls.

But that was just one of the risks of being a rotten show-off.

He sort of swaggered through the door and stood there looking expressionlessly down at McReadie's body while the other Arab levered himself off the bunk and yawned. Abdul jangled over and, jerking his head at the inert Commander, said something to his oppo. The jailer shrugged and turned towards me and, after untying me, jerked me unresistingly to my feet and pushed me violently towards the door.

I had one sickening, macabre vision of the hood with the high explosive jewellery slapping and slapping at the lolling head of a dead man, then my bloke gave me another shove which sent me crashing against the bulkhead on the other side of the internal alleyway.

I suppose the sight of me sobbing with the fresh

agony from my injured shoulder must have injected him with a surge of power sadism because I had one terror-struck vision of blackly contemptuous eyes behind the butt of his gun as it swung up to smash down on the unprotected side of my head.

Or at least, it would have done.

If McReadie's bloodstained arm hadn't hooked around his throat and, with utterly satisfying viciousness, yanked him backwards into the cabin again.

*

I just stared and stared at the receding gunman with uncomprehending eyes. McReadie . . . ? And not only alive but – there was a choking shriek as our late jailer clutched at his crotch – but *kicking*?

Slowly I started to get mad at McReadie. All the time I'd been slapped around on that bloody bridge of Hosni's he'd lain there on the deck, as relaxed and comfortable as he would have been on a luxury cruise liner. . . . And the way he'd counterfeited death for the last anticipation-filled hours. Without even once giving me the moral support which might have eased my nightmarish loneliness. . . . But, suddenly, I caught sight of his waxen, drawn features, sectored by the black rivulets of dried blood, and began to imagine just a tiny bit of the agony his tortured, voluntarily paralysed body must have endured as it craved for the relief of movement . . .

. . . then McReadie himself came hurtling out of the

cabin and, slamming the door shut, yelled, 'Down, Cable . . . ! Five . . . six . . . seven . . .'

I watched foolishly and wondered why he was holding on to the door handle like that when all the men inside needed to do was pick themselves up, untangle their S.M.G.'s and . . .

McReadie's eyes were wild in the black hollows of his skull. And he was still counting. That was another bloody silly thing to be doing, counting instead of running. Then someone inside the room started battering on the door in terror, and tugging frantically at the handle. And I just couldn't think why they were whimpering like that, either.

Until McReadie howled, '. . . TEN! Get *down* f'r Chrissake! I jus' throat chopped him an' flicked the pin out've . . .'

He let go of the door handle and hit me low with his shoulder while he was still screaming '. . . *Grenaaaaade!*'

We were twelve feet from the cabin door when Abdul the Magnificent started to blow up.

*

It must have been one of the Mills grenades that went first, judging by the characteristic *crish-crash* as the detonator exploded milli-seconds before the main charge. I didn't waste too long on a connoisseur's assessment though because, by the time the first blast slammed the door off its hinges on the end of a long jet of flame, I was busy lying flat on the deck alongside

McReadie and both of us trying to dig our way through the compo screed below us.

By then the late Abdul must have been bouncing around the blistering steel walls of the cabin like a huge Catherine Wheel as the rest of his belt load blew in a chain reaction which pounded and battered unbearably at our bursting eardrums.

I felt the tatters of the uniform shirt on my back start to smoulder under the lick of the super-heated blasts deflecting crazily along the funnel of the alleyway while, a million miles away, I could hear myself crying uncontrollably with the shock of it all.

And even when the flamboyant death of an extrovert had ended on a last shattering eruption which could only have been the Soviet RPG-43, and the steel walls of the midship section incandesced to a dull white heat and peeled out towards us while the burns on my legs graduated from third degree to second degree, I could still hear a screaming above me which went on and on and on.

But it was only the *Ayacucho City*'s siren shrieking in perplexed outrage under the hands of some terrified Arab watchkeeper. Otherwise, everything was terribly quiet and still. For a few, stunned moments.

Painfully slowly McReadie dragged himself to his knees and hovered over me, with the acrid wreaths of cordite forming little puff-curls around the mask of a face.

And he grinned. The bloody idiot actually grinned.

Then said, 'You've been relaxing too long, Cable

boy. Now let's go an' *really* wake the bastards up. Just you and me . . . with *British Commander.*'

*

I even stopped sobbing from the starfish spurts of agony vectoring into my nervous system from every extremity. I'd been, to say the least, mildly surprised when McReadie had suddenly risen from the ashes of hope and, like an avenging Phoenix, had kindled a flame of retribution under Abdul's T.N.T. waistcoat.

But now he wanted to go and start fighting everyone else as well. It suggested an aggressive streak which wasn't quite nice, but that was the trouble with being British – we have to keep on going to the last battle, just so's we can bloody well win one.

Except that McReadie and I had about as much chance of winning our current conflict as Hosni had of being elected Premier of Israel. And anyway . . .

I shook my head experimentally. 'The excitement's de-magnetised your compass, McReadie. We don't *have* a bloody ship any more, remember?'

He shrugged enigmatically and winced as he forced himself the rest of the way to his feet. 'Half a loaf, old boy . . .'

Which I thought at the time was a damned silly platitude, but I didn't say much because I had to show a little appreciation for his saving me from a fate worse than death. Now I just had the death bit to face up to instead.

And in about sixty seconds from now, according to

the sounds of running feet and hoarsely shouted
commands which came from the starboard alleyway.

McReadie bent down and, placing his hands under
my arms, hauled me roughly to my feet. There always
seemed to be somebody pulling me around aboard the
Ayacucho City. Then he gave me a not too gentle shove
towards the head of the internal stairway leading to the
forward lower decks, and gritted urgently, 'Let's go,
Cable! And fast. . . .'

So we went.

We went with the white heat from the crematorium
licking across our faces and the hair frizzing away to
nothing on our unprotected heads. Because the only
way we could avoid running into the guns of the rest of
Hosni's crowd was to pass the glowing hole of the once
cabin entrance. And as I started to cough and choke on
the thickening fumes I only remembered just in time
that, if I drew even one breath of that incinerating air
into my screaming lungs, then Brevet Cable would
never come out of the other side . . .

. . . and then I was through, and retching against the
cool brass rail of the stairway, and not really caring
whether McReadie would make it or not, until he came
charging out of the smoke like a two-year-old bloody
greyhound and kept right on going past me and down
the stairs, yelling, 'What the hell're you waiting for,
Cable . . . ?'

Which made me so mad I roared back down at him,
'For you to tell me where I'm fuggin' *going*, McReadie!
Only for that!'

His face looked very flushed as he looked back from the foot of the stairs. Or maybe it was just the burns. But I'll never forget the way his eyes glinted from the shadows like Devil's candles, or the controlled excitement in his flat voice as he shouted back.

'I said – "half a loaf", Cable. Well, we've got our half mounted right across Hosni's bows. And the last time I saw her she still had a machine gun rigged, out on her port wing. . . .'

I didn't hear the rest, because he'd gone. And I didn't want to be alone. Not anymore.

We started running for the crazy black silhouette which reared skeletally against the night sky. It didn't even look like *Commander*'s bridge now, not the way her wheelhouse windows gaped like so many decayed teeth, and the canted, immobile radar antennae stared wistfully astern to where there'd once been a beautiful funnel, and a trim ship, and a house flag with a lion on it. . . .

But we weren't house proud either, right then.

We were just thinking about a lot of little children, waiting for Santa Claus!

*

They didn't see us until we were nearly back aboard our own ridiculous splinter of ship.

The port wing loomed over me, enormously high in the darkness, and I nervously watched McReadie's backside disappearing over the wooden rail as he clambered inboard, then I was struggling to haul

239

myself up over the port sidelight screen with my feet slipping on the polished brass of the lamp itself.

For one nonsensical moment I thought, 'Don't smash the glass for God's sake, Cable, or you'll have a bit of explaining to do to the Shore Superinten . . .'

Then I remembered I was going to have to explain how we'd broken the other 99 per cent of J.C.'s boat anyway, and suddenly it didn't seem too important.

Curiously, when I stretched out my hand to grip the bracket that still supported the white ring of a lifebuoy marked BRITISH COMMANDER. LONDON, it rather disconcertingly disappeared, then the buoy itself dissolved into a haze of cork chips and wildly snaking grab line while I stared foolishly at the diagonal line of bullet holes running parallel to, and four inches under, my groping arm.

Above me McReadie murmured irritably, 'Bugger it! They've seen us.' But I was too busy scrabbling for another handhold to tell him I bloody knew *that* much already.

He leaned over the rail, grabbed a handful of the seat of my shorts, and we were both sprawled on the inboard side of the bridge wing listening to the drum of nine millimetre fire on the armour plated shield between us and the marksman.

When they stopped, thirty shells and an empty magazine later, McReadie grinned savagely and tugged at the concealing canvas jacket over the machine gun. 'Right!' he gritted with an irritating happiness I couldn't quite match under the circumstances, 'Right!

So now let's find out if *they've* got a steel plated bloody wheelhouse too, eh.'

I carefully raised my head over the line of the rail and saw that, even apart from us, Hosni had other troubles as well. The fire that we'd left in the centrecastle accommodation had started to spread outwards and upwards, jetting through the steel rimmed port and across the boat deck in great licks of flame, then curling higher to send sparks twisting and glinting up into the black night like a hundred thousand comets.

One last glimpse of the great yellow funnel flickering like a sickly gasometer in the dancing reflections, and the long low shape of her bridge and wheelhouse picked out in all the autumn tints of red, then McReadie was slamming the cocking handle of the machine gun back to the 'Fire' position while his forefinger curled around the trigger. . . .

For a few moments I lay listening to the slam of the gun over my head, and feeling the hot, gleaming little brass cylinders of the expended rounds tinkling down around me, then I pushed my eyes up over the rail again and couldn't help grinning with the savage excitement of it all.

I found out they didn't have an armoured bridge front for a start – just an ordinary, wooden sheathed one. McReadie's first long burst chopped horizontally across from port to starboard and I just watched, and grinned wider and wider, as the varnished teak boards sprang from their frames in perfect sequence, right across the bridge, like a line of chorus girls going into one of those arms linked, high kick routines.

Then McReadie bent fractionally at the knees, angling the air-cooled barrel slightly higher, and he was traversing back over to port while the geometrically precise squares of *their* wheelhouse windows disintegrated in a smashing cataract of plexiglass splinters and flying wood slivers.

When the machine gun stopped it seemed as though a blanket of silence had been drawn over our heads. Only the shuddering throb of the straining engines and the soft swish of the sea dragging past the crippled bow below us relieved the stillness.

I raised my eyes and watched the yellow moon as it hovered just above the foremasthead. It was quiet up there, too. Quiet and cold, and dead. Like an anthrax-contaminated corpse. . . .

Like my brief excitement was cold and dead also.

I wondered if Hosni had been caught in that withering burst of fire, the way their helmsman must have been. It didn't really make much difference, because I'd suddenly remembered the one thing which made all this arrogant, thin red line and salute the Colours defiance of ours into a futile, irrelevant gesture – the final spitting of a wounded wildcat before the shotgun blasts in its snarling face.

For I remembered the flash from the night on the *Ayacucho City*'s foc'slehead – this foc'slehead. And, later, while *Commander* was swinging crazily under her last helm order, the sight of a man running along the Liberian's boat deck with a curious tube over his shoulder, and my dismissing it as irrelevant . . . until McReadie's shocked features at the wheelhouse door of a dying ship screamed, 'They had a fuggin' gun, Cable! You never said they had a fug . . . !'

But they did. Except that they were more sophisticated than that because they had a rocket launcher. Which could slice through a sheet of armour plate like a kiddie's finger through the icing of a birthday cake. And I knew that much without guessing – because I could still see where it had already done so, just before it tore away a captain's head, a helmsman's chest and a slim young second mate's reason. . . .

McReadie grinned into the darkness above me. 'She's out of control, Cable. Or maybe Hosni can't get another freedom fighting volunteer to take over the wheel.'

I took another glance at the moon and suddenly it did seem to be slipping sideways, away from the dim spire of the mast. I just felt all flat and dead inside, though, not at all vindictive or sad, or happy or even frightened anymore. I knew they wouldn't even have to connect up the nice, sheltered emergency steering position on the poop, not while they could laugh at us over the sights of that bloody rocket.

Without warning the deck under our feet stopped vibrating and the stillness grew even more intense. I muttered dully, 'They've stopped engines.'

McReadie swung the gun barrel experimentally.

'Clever people, you Chief Officers. To know a technical thing like that . . . Got a cigarette left, old boy?'

I shook my head, not really hearing him. I was trying to make up my mind whether to remind him about the rocket launcher, or just let him go on believing we could keep Hosni pinned down for ever aboard this shipload of death – until, unaware of what must come, the old McReadie grin vanished in a last, uncomprehending blaze of white hot steel shards.

Then he looked down at me and smiled very softly, and said, 'A pity. About the cigarettes. It would have been nice to have had a last smoke together . . . before they hit us with that bloody awful rocket up there.'

We gazed at each other for quite a long time, with the flames from the boat deck roaring and leaping high into the black sky. But not even the fire was enough to stop Hosni, all it could do would be to burn out the upper decks, maybe even the wheelhouse, and cause the Israelis to believe even more devoutly in the utter generosity of God while the golden ears of grain still swung out of our undamaged holds. . . .

I realised then that I'd loved McReadie like a brother under all our cynical sniping. But it was too late for love now, because hate had taken over in our isolated world and I was just being old fashioned, so I dropped my eyes in embarrassment and muttered awkwardly, 'There should be a Verey pistol in what's left of the chart room. I'll get it. Perhaps another ship might raise us.'

I started to crawl away when something stopped me.

I turned to see him watching. When he spoke his voice sounded so gentle.

'There might be a lifebelt in there too, Brev. Why don't you just slide over into the water? You've got the kind of luck it needs for a story book ending . . . and I've got the gun to see they don't come looking too soon.'

I blinked wetly in the darkness, then started crawling again. 'Get stuffed, McReadie!' I threw over my shoulder.

But I didn't really mean it!

Then – suddenly – all the violence and hate and terror was slamming in on us again as the submachine guns winked along the *Ayacucho City*'s great white ghost of a centrecastle, and McReadie was screaming 'Geddown Cable boy! F'r Chrissake keep your head down . . . !' while his hunched shoulders absorbed the shuddering recoil of the heavy machine gun as it snarled back in lonely contempt . . .

. . . but I just knelt where I was, and didn't attempt to move because it didn't matter any more anyway, and listened to the crack of the fire coning in on us above the shrieking keen of ricocheting bullets . . . and watched McReadie's tracers ever so slowly arc away to sparkle prettily against the steel face of the ship.

I was glad we'd done it this way. There was a lot more to see than when you were just drowning.

Until the first rocket exploded exactly on my nice, red, shiny port sidelight.

And our beautiful machine gun spiralled fifty feet

into the air among all the frisking ruby sparks, before it fell away into the dark sea where our bows should have been, but weren't.

While good old McReadie hurtled backwards on the perimeter of the blast with an expression of intense shock on his face. And the front of his scalp curling up over his skull like a ridiculous, gleaming quiff.

Armageddon

They didn't fire again. They probably saw they didn't need to as the roaring flames flickered from the high boat deck, washing the silent, twisted piece of a dead ship with all the reds and browns of the spectrum.

I didn't do much either, not for a very long time. I just knelt there on that amputated bridge and held McReadie's cold, limp hand, and felt very sad.

I cried a little, too, though I wasn't really sure whether it was for myself, or McReadie, or all the dead men of *Commander*, or for a faceless host of doomed children . . . and as the first tear splashed on the scarred deck it started to tremble gently, then the pulse of the ship grew stronger as her screws threshed hugely, dragging the stern once again through the water.

And the moon slowly slid back to its hook above the foremast while we settled on our ridiculous, backward course towards Haifa and the end of the world.

I wondered what they'd say about the bullet scars and the cordite stains around me, and the blackened, gutted shell of her upperworks. But I knew Hosni would have a story – of pirates and collisions and violence, yes. But the characters would assume a new identity, and the motives twist out of all recognition. And the funny thing was that they'd believe him far more easily than if they knew the utterly fantastic, incredible truth.

So the tugboats would gather round the heroic freighter as she limped into Haifa Roads, and President Anwar Sadat's representatives would smile proudly and positively swell with the happiness of giving generously. And the relief trucks would line up at the distribution points. . . .

Or maybe a man called J.C. would make a telephone call. Just because he was a human being. And the outraged tank engines would roar along the Suez Canal instead, while the Star of David fighter bombers would jink through the radar screens round Cairo, and Amman, and Damascus.

And the Soviet Mediterranean Fleet, and all the sleek grey warships of N.A.T.O., would go over to Nuclear Condition Red. . . .

I was glad when I heard them coming for me, carefully picking their way through the shambles of the *Ayacucho City*'s well deck. Gently I folded McReadie's arms across his chest and stood up. I didn't want to wait too long.

In case I started crying again.

*

There were four of them below me, Hosni and the girl and, straddle legged behind them, the silhouettes of two commandos.

When they saw me they didn't move for a minute. I didn't move either, I just clung to the charred wooden

rail and felt the fresh blood running down into my eyes,
and listened to the little voice in my head screaming,
'Tell them to get it over with, Cable. F'r Chrissake,
beg them to . . . Go right down on your bloody knees an'
pray you get it in the head. . . .'

Hosni stepped forward and I looked at the gun with
the fold-over shoulder stock and the burr walnut grip.
Then the girl moved up beside him and they stood
there together with the dancing flames reflecting back
into their faces. They looked a very ordinary, nice
couple. Very handsome and sincere. I didn't really hate
them at all, because he was only a patriot . . . and you
can't hate a girl with such a bloody lovely pair of
legs. . . .

Hosni said quietly, 'I'm sorry, Cable. You were both
very brave. I really am sorry . . . !'

I didn't feel at all frightened when his gun muzzle
came up towards my head. I didn't even register how
big and black and sad the girl's eyes were.

Because I was staring past them, aft towards the
centrecastle, to where a great white finger of atomised
spray slowly rose two hundred feet into the air and hung,
incredibly suspended, over the *Ayacucho City*'s shattered
bridge.

And it wasn't until the column of water finally
collapsed – along with bits of lifeboat and ship's rail,
and steel plate and firefighting Arab pirates, and the
ship started to roll over to starboard with sickening
finality – that I eventually realised what had happened.

That we had been hit.

By a torpedo.

I never saw the two gunmen again, only the shiny smear across the steel deck and through the smashed bulwarks left by the five ton forward derrick after it had slipped from its cradle and swept them both into the sea.

I didn't see a great deal more of Hosni and the girl either. Just one brief flash of their two bodies clinging together in the red glow as he stared wildly round and tried to understand why his dream could never come true.

Then the moon gave the foretopmast a sly push and it fell lazily out of the black sky. I tried not to look where it landed, but I had to – and all I could see projecting from the concave lip of the crater was a beautifully polished burr walnut gleam, and . . . a pair of legs.

But they weren't lovely, though. Not any more.

The deck under my feet canted and I heard the tortured metal shrieking below as the bridge I was standing on tried to free itself from the listing *Ayacucho City*. I still didn't move because I was spellbound by the sight of the great yellow funnel I'd spent so many million years in as it lay further and further over, with the roaring, excited flames peeling the skin off it in blazing, floating shreds.

Then the ship gave another agonised heave and we

lay over to thirty degrees, and the funnel couldn't stand it any longer so it toppled ever so slowly down into the inferno then rolled thunderously over the side just as I turned dazedly to watch the cold sea tumbling enormously inboard to swamp up the sloping deck towards me . . .

. . . and an obscene, blood red skull with a ridiculous flap of skin waving loosely, said dryly, 'Christ, but you made a helluva job of that on your own, mate!'

*

We jumped together, McReadie and I, and it was only because we went over her fore-end that we avoided being dragged down with her as she rolled right under thirty seconds later, with her engines ripping from their bed plates like a submarine avalanche and her hatches bursting open in great sobbing gouts of liberated air. And grain.

There were two other survivors – both badly shocked – but they died very quickly, with their lungs full of water. Oh, we had to help just a little but then we also had to keep our secret, as McReadie had emphasised earlier. It still wasn't nice, though I didn't mind too much with mine – he wore white engineer's overalls and, after all, it *was* my turn to try and kill him anyway. And without the aid of a machine gun from the bottom of an endless flight of ladders.

I suppose the most difficult part of surviving was trying to avoid swallowing any of the contaminated grain which was starting to well up around us from the

Liberian's collapsing holds far below. But that would soon be neutralised by the hugeness of the sea.

The motor torpedo boat picked us up twenty minutes later. It was only when I saw the ensign with the Shield of David in its centre that I realised that at least one commander in the Israeli Navy didn't want the war to end either. I found out a little later that the Zionist-Arab love bubble had already started to fracture during the last few days, now that the initial shock had worn off – maybe Hosni had even guessed it would all the time.

Either way, all it had needed was for one un-disciplined hawk from the other side – the Jewish 'torpedoes speak louder than diplomats' fraternity – to be patrolling the Haifa Approaches when the *Ayacucho City* clawed invitingly sternwards under the tubes of his unemployed M.T.B. and . . . well, one uncontrollable, trigger-happy patriot's much the same as another, and sinking the Egyptian's gift did seem a pretty effective way of preventing an Arab-Israeli reconciliation?

It was a bit poetic, all the same, though the grim-faced kids lining the torpedo boat's rail couldn't understand why I couldn't stop bloody laughing. But I knew McReadie would. Oh, I knew McReadie would. . . .

The last impression I had before they dragged me from the water was that we were floating on a golden yellow carpet. But it was only grain.

And even that would be gone before the sun rose again over the Promised Land.